Because of her faith, Marji Parker left the comfort and security of her wealthy family for the sordid world of the Lower East Side, hoping to bring God's love to desperately darkened lives. But in order to do her work, Marji had to live constantly with danger. Her new world never allowed her to relax, never gave her the luxury of trusting the people she met day by day. And yet Marji learned to cope. Even more, she was able to carry out her vital work in this hostile environment. If your life has problems ... barriers ... fears ... learn Marji's secret of success and peace.

BY John Benton

She risked life itself
to prevent bloodshed.

MARJI
and the Gangland Wars

John Benton

NEW HOPE
BOOKS

Fleming H. Revell Company
Old Tappan, New Jersey

Scripture quotations in this volume are from the King James Version of the Bible.

ISBN:0-8007-8407-3
A New Hope Book
Copyright © 1981 by John Benton
All rights reserved
Printed in the United States of America
This is an original New Hope Book, published by
New Hope Books, a division of Fleming H. Revell
Company, Old Tappan, New Jersey.

TO Nancy Jerdon,
a very special friend
to Elsie and me

Whether it is walking the streets
looking for the lost or
counseling a troubled girl in
our office, Nancy's love
knows no limits to lift a fallen girl.

MARJI

and the Gangland Wars

Synopsis

What happens when a girl from one of the wealthiest families on Long Island decides to open a Christian mission in a ghetto—and in the Lower East Side at that, a place described by some as the "armpit of the world"?

How does such a girl—a college graduate, raised with luxury and wealth as constant companions, training to take over her father's successful Parker Manufacturing Company—relate to prostitutes, pimps, drug addicts, alcoholics, purveyors of pornography, and people who have given up on life? How could she possibly live among the stench, the filth, the crime?

Marji Parker didn't choose her work through a series of vocational aptitude tests. In fact, she stumbled into it through what some might say was a quirk of fate. But she would be quick to tell you it really was "directed by the Lord."

Marji had become a born-again Christian while in college. She looked for a special way to serve her Lord, but nothing seemed quite right.

One night, after attending a gospel concert, Marji was to spend the night with her aunt in her fashionable apartment on the East Side of New York City. In the elevator on the way up to her aunt's apartment, Marji was accosted by a teenage boy who had two things on his mind: robbery and rape.

He forced her onto the roof of the apartment building, rifled her purse for money, and grabbed her. Marji breathed a quick prayer and, as she would express it, "With the help of the Lord, I talked him out of his evil intentions."

But in the course of talking to the would-be rapist, Marji became aware of the terrible hopelessness of people like him. She tried to tell him there was hope in God, but he didn't believe what she was saying. And then he uttered those words which were destined to change the course of Marji's life and to echo through her mind forever: "Where is your God in the ghetto?"

She had no answer which would satisfy him—or herself. That night, after reading a book about the Walter Hoving Home in Garrison, New York, and John and Elsie Benton's ministry to seemingly hopeless girls, she decided to open a Christian mission on the Lower East Side in an attempt to take the news of Christ's love and concern to the people who lived there.

Her parents, of course, were aghast. Neither Harry nor Mary Parker were Christians, and they couldn't see their attractive, capable daughter throwing her life away on what they considered worthless scum.

But then came the revelation that her dad's brother, Alex, whom Marji thought was a successful businessman in Germany, was really an alcoholic her father was supporting on the Lower East Side. That revelation helped change her parents' attitude, especially when Uncle Alex agreed that Marji could live with him and his wife, Amilda.

Marji quickly found that an outsider has to earn the trust of the people on the Lower East Side. She kept her wealthy background a secret for a while. But evil forces continually tried to thwart her program. She was almost killed when a bomb exploded in the counseling center she had finally managed to open next door to a pornography shop. But that experience became the turning point in the community's somewhat reluctant acceptance of the rich girl. And through it, her aunt and uncle both became Christians.

Marji's mother did, too. And when she came to visit Marji in her chauffeured limousine, the news began to get around that Marji was rich. And that indirectly led to people thinking in terms of kidnapping—a story told in the book *Marji and the Kidnap Plot*.

By this time, Marji has helped a number of girls in the area to see their need for a Saviour and to forsake their sinful lives. These girls have gone to the Walter Hoving Home and developed into strong Christians.

Marji helps the people who cannot leave the area through Bible studies in her counseling center and practical assistance with their everyday needs. The counseling-center ministry has continued to grow gradually. And Marji Parker has become a well-known part of New York City's Lower East Side.

1

I knew I shouldn't be out on the streets of the Lower East Side of New York City this late at night. No woman in her right mind should be. But what else could I do?

For one thing, I was still basking in the glow of the wonderful privilege I had just had—that of leading a prostitute to accept Jesus as her Saviour at my counseling center. It was absolutely thrilling, when she finally realized that Jesus had indeed made her a new creation. But it took her a long time to realize that. The poor girl had been abused at an early age. She had a self-image that bordered on zero. She found it hard to see how anybody—including God—could care about her.

When she finally realized the truth, she wanted to rejoice and rejoice and rejoice. So we did!

But now I was out here on the street later than I should have been. It was a good thing it was only a couple of blocks to the apartment I shared with my Uncle Alex and Aunt Amilda.

I silently asked the Lord to care for me, but I quickened my pace. My sixth sense told me something strange was going on. Nothing really looked unusual—I saw the customary cars up and down the street and a few other people around. Yet I had this unexplained uneasiness.

I had learned that whenever I got into a situation like this, I needed to ask God to cover me with the blood of Jesus. Oh, how thankful I was that the blood He shed not only provided forgiveness for our sins but also became our protection from evil!

But still the fear persisted. Was I about to be mugged by some junkie who needed money for a fix? Or would some maniac grab me and rape me?

My stomach felt tied in knots, and I was almost running now. What was this strange force compelling me? Why was I so terrified? I'd been on this street hundreds of times before and—

My reasoning was interrupted in the middle of a thought as I turned a corner and came face-to-face with a gang member!

I gasped in surprise and terror. He stood there defiantly, his legs spread apart and his switchblade thrust out toward me, within striking distance!

"Don't try to run, preacher lady!" he warned. "I won't hurt you if you do as I say."

He called me "preacher lady." That meant he knew about me. But what did he know? And who was he? I didn't remember ever having seen him before.

"What do you want?" I asked, far more calmly than I felt.

He didn't answer. Instead, he threw his left arm around me and spun me around. Then he jabbed the knife at my throat. "I said, preacher lady, you start to squirm or yell, and I'll slash you hard! There'll be blood all over this place!"

"Listen, young man, let's not play games. What do you want?"

"My old lady is starving at home. She doesn't have any food. Somebody stole her welfare check. I heard you helped people."

Sure I helped people. But was this a setup? I'd gotten food for a lot of hungry people on the Lower East Side, but I sure had never been approached in this way before!

"Okay," I said, "so your mother is at home and

needs food. Now before I make a move, why don't you tell me who you are?"

"Shut up!" he muttered. "You think I'm dumb? The less you know about me, the less you can tell the cops."

He might have known I was the "preacher lady," but obviously he didn't know much else about me. I had quickly learned that I didn't dare run to the cops with every little problem or threat I had had. I knew that if I did that, I'd soon ruin my effectiveness in this area. People here thought the cops were their enemies, and they sure wouldn't trust me if they thought I was working with the police.

"Okay, okay. I won't ask any more questions about you. But tell me—how did you know about me?"

"Preacher lady," he laughed, "everybody down here knows about you and your counseling center. We know how you are pulling prostitutes off the street. We know how you help junkies. We know how Benny Barnes, that mean old pimp, tried to kill you. And that story about your being kidnapped—that was in all the papers. And we all know from that that your old man is filthy rich."

"Hey, come off that one," I interrupted. "I can't help it that I was born into a rich family."

"And neither can I help it that I was born not knowing who my father is," the teenager said. "I couldn't help it that I was thrown out of the house when I was ten years old. But I could help it when I became president of the Tattooed Terrors. I fought my way to the top of that gang, and I don't fear man or beast. And I'm sure not scared of you!"

"Oh, you don't need to be afraid of me," I said, "especially when you keep that knife up against my throat. You've got my word that I'm not going to try anything."

"Okay, I'll pull the knife away. Then we're going to walk along the street. If the cops see us together, you're going to play it cool. Understand?"

I breathed easier as he put his switchblade away.

"Is anybody following you?" he wanted to know.

"There sure is," I answered. "I mean, all the time I've been walking down this street there—"

I knew I'd said the wrong thing because he flipped out his switchblade and put it to my throat again. "Where are they?" he demanded.

"Look straight above you. Right up there."

He took the knife away from my throat as he craned this way and that. Finally he said, "I can't see anybody."

"You can't? Look again."

He peered up at the roofs of the tenements that surrounded us. Still unable to see anybody, he turned back to me and said, "Listen, preacher lady, if that friend of yours gets within a hundred feet of me, I'll kill you. You'd better warn him!"

I smiled. "You'll never know how close my friends are because you can't see them: they're angels," I explained. "God sends His angels to guard me. You can't see them, but they're there!"

"I guess I should have expected something nutty like that," he grunted. "They say on the street that you're kind of a freak about this religion bit. I don't have any time for it, myself. But my old lady is sick and needs help. So you'd better come with me now. And let's not have any more of that spooky angel talk."

He grabbed my arm and started yanking. I had no choice but to follow.

We got up to East Twelfth Street. I realized anew that my work down here seemed to make so little difference. The Lower East Side was getting worse every day. More burned-out buildings. More garbage on the streets. More muggings. More killings. More rapes. When would it all end?

As he led me into an old tenement, I said, "Listen, you're not trying to set me up or anything, are you?"

"Preacher lady, I don't blame you for not trusting me.

Not many people do. But I've got things straightened out with my mom, and I really do care about her. She's the only one I have left. My two older brothers are in jail. My sister is a junkie and hasn't been home in two years. And my little brother got killed in a gang war. So Mom is the only family I have left."

My heart went out to him. Oh, the sorrow and suffering in this place. It made me mad at the devil once again for leading people astray and creating ghettos like this.

"What's your name, son?" I asked as gently as I could.

"Preacher lady, you sure ask a lot of questions. I'll tell you, if you don't ask any more. My name is Ratface."

Through the light coming out the door of the tenement, I saw him for the first time. He had two lines tattooed across each side of the lower part of his face—to represent whiskers, I guess. And they did make him look like a rat. But I also knew that underneath this disguise was a teenager who desperately needed God's forgiveness.

Just as we stepped into the tenement, Ratface grabbed my arm. "Hold it!" he whispered.

He peered up the stairs. "Somebody is up there," he whispered. "I can feel him."

"Is this where you live?" I whispered back.

"Yes. Up on the fourth floor. The rent is cheaper up there. But that's part of the problem: My old lady has a hard time getting up and down these stairs."

He peered up the stairs again. "Can I trust you?" he asked.

"Of course you can trust me. But can I trust you?"

"You can trust me," Ratface said. "I have a feeling something is wrong up there, so I want you to stay here. Let me walk a little way up those stairs by myself."

He pulled out his switchblade, flicked it open and, holding it in front of him, slowly ascended, looking from side to side. I watched.

Just as he got to the top of those stairs, a door opened. Ratface sprang into the air. I heard a woman scream and slam the door. That made chills run up and down my back.

"That wasn't it," Ratface half whispered down to me. "There's something else."

He turned the corner, out of my sight. That's when I heard a man's voice scream, "Got you covered, Ratface! Drop that knife! Drop it right where you are!"

I took the steps two at a time and got to the spot where I could see what looked like a junkie holding a gun on Ratface. The junkie acted as though I weren't even there.

"Ratface, you and me are going to take a little trip," the junkie announced.

Ratface had his hands up in the air, but he hadn't dropped his knife yet.

"I told you to drop that knife!" the junkie bellowed. "Do it now, or I'll blast your guts!"

The knife clattered to the floor.

"What are you going to do with me, man?" Ratface asked. "I've never hurt you."

"Of course you never hurt me," the junkie said. "But I heard there's five thousand bucks waiting for anybody who delivers you alive to the Hidden Skulls. Man, I need that money. I'm going to get a mountain of drugs with that money."

"You're crazy, man," Ratface told him. "Those Hidden Skulls won't give you money. They don't have that kind of money around."

"That's what you think!" the junkie replied. "You're going with me, and I'm going to collect my reward."

"You're crazy, man!" Ratface protested. "They'll kill you!"

Ignoring the threat, the junkie motioned Ratface to start down the stairs. He followed, the gun trained on Ratface's head. I tried to melt into the wall as Ratface walked by me on the stairs, suddenly looking very small and helpless. Oh, how I wanted to do something. But what?

As the junkie passed me, something came over me, and I jabbed my little finger into his back. "Say your prayers!" I threatened. "It's all over. Drop that gun!"

The junkie threw his arms up and his gun down in one motion. I grabbed his gun and pointed it at him. "Don't try anything, or I'll have to blast the nose off your face."

I couldn't believe I was saying things like that! It was totally out of character for me. But maybe it was because I was so terrified.

"Lady, lady, please don't kill me!" the junkie pleaded. "I didn't mean anybody any harm."

"Get out that door and out of my sight!" I screamed. "Now!"

He bounded down the steps, out the door, and hit the pavement on the run, his legs churning like crazy.

No sooner had the junkie disappeared than Ratface asked, "Where's your other gun?"

I smiled. "I didn't have any gun at his back. I just used my finger."

"You did what?" he asked, aghast. "You must be absolutely crazy!"

"I guess you're right. It was a stupid thing to do. If he had turned around, he would have been aware I was bluffing. He probably would have killed me."

As I said that, I guess the reality of what I had done began to sink in. My knees started to shake, and I felt light-headed. The last thing I remember was that I was starting to fall forward.

I don't know how long I was out. Suddenly I became aware that someone was gently slapping my face. I tried to focus my eyes, and realized I was looking up at Ratface.

"Where am I?" I asked.

"You're in my mom's apartment. I carried you upstairs. Are you okay?"

I tried to sit up, but my head felt as though it were splitting. I finally managed, with great difficulty, to pull myself into a sitting position.

Across the room, sitting in a big chair, was an older woman.

"My goodness, young lady," she said, "when my son carried you in here, I didn't know what to think. You're too beautiful to be a member of his gang. Are you a prostitute or something?"

"Mom," Ratface interrupted, "this is the preacher lady I was telling you about. Maybe she can help you. Mom, she just saved my life. She must be okay."

I felt my strength returning, so I lifted myself onto a nearby chair. "Preacher lady," Ratface said, "whatever you want from me, you can have. I guess I'd be asking too much now for you to help my mom out with food. I feel so ashamed of the way I treated you tonight. As soon as you feel like it, I'll walk you back to your apartment."

"Ratface, you and I have to learn to like each other," I said. "That was God who helped us out of that predicament down there. And I know He had a reason for it." He grinned.

"And of course I'm going to help your mother," I went on. "That's why I'm down here—to help people."

I looked over at her and saw that she had her head down, trying to muffle her sobs. I walked over, knelt beside her, and asked gently, "Mother, what do you need?"

"I'm too ashamed to tell you."

"Come on, Mother. I'll do the best I can. I understand you don't have any food at all."

I walked into the kitchen, and roaches scattered everywhere. I checked the cupboards. They were absolutely bare—except for roaches. I checked the refrigerator. Nothing.

"Well, let's start with some food," I said. "And it doesn't look as though this can wait until morning. We'll do it now. I'll be right back."

"Where you going?" Ratface asked.

"To my apartment. I'll gather a few things. Then tomorrow, I'll go to the grocery store and buy you and your mother some staples. It sure looks as though you need some."

Ratface walked back to my apartment with me. Aunt Amilda and I put a few things together for him to take back to his mother. "See you tomorrow," I told him.

The next morning, Amilda and I went to the grocery store. We bought four big bags of groceries and carried them to Ratface's mother. He was still there. He almost seemed surprised to see us.

I didn't wait around for any thanks. After all, I was doing this in the name of Jesus. I knew He was keeping score. But as I started out of the door, Ratface said, "Preacher lady, whenever you need a favor, let me know. I owe you one."

Suddenly, I had an idea. "Ratface, why don't you and your gang meet me tomorrow night at my counseling center on East Eleventh Street? I'm also going to invite the Hidden Skulls. I want to talk to both gangs together."

"Preacher lady, you're crazy!" Ratface exploded. "If we get in the same place with those Hidden Skulls, there is going to be war!"

"I know that," I replied. "But I also know there won't be any war if you both decide not to have war. Well, you asked if you could do something for me. That's what I'd really like. But I'll leave it up to you."

"Okay. I said I owe you one. I'll try it. I'll send the word to my guys. They'll be there if I tell them to come. You check with the Hidden Skulls. But there's one thing you have to emphasize to them: Everybody has to stay cool! I mean, real cool!"

"I assure you nothing will happen, Ratface."

"You and me have to be on the level on this one, preacher lady. This isn't fun and games. And don't you think for one minute about calling any cops. Just remember, if anything goes wrong, there are going to be killings. And I sure can't guarantee your safety if you set us up!"

"You've got my word, Ratface: no cops. And I believe God will see to it that everything goes all right."

Aunt Amilda and I headed home, my head filled with grandiose ideas about doing something to stop these stupid gang wars. But at that moment I had no earthly idea what I was getting into!

I did know that the Hidden Skulls and the Tattooed Terrors were the worst of the gangs in the area. The territory of the Hidden Skulls was south of East Eleventh: the territory of the Tattooed Terrors was northeast of Eleventh. My counseling center was on Eleventh Street—a logical neutral meeting place.

For the past three weeks, the war between these two gangs had been especially bad. Teenagers in both gangs had been killed. The Hidden Skulls had lost at least five of their members, and the Tattooed Terrors had lost seven. Sometimes they battled right in front of my counseling center!

Later that day, I went to the president of the Hidden Skulls. He was skeptical, but finally agreed to the truce. He also warned me about the police. I assured him there would be no police. I simply wanted both gangs to talk and to stop the war.

The night of the meeting, I started to my counseling center early so I could spend some time in prayer. I knew nothing about ending gang wars. If peace were to come, it would have to come from the Lord.

When I was a few feet away from the door of the center, I noticed something gray hanging from a string on the door handle. Then I saw something red splattered all over the door. As I got closer, I realized someone had brutally stabbed a huge rat, spread its blood all over the door, and tied the filthy thing onto my door. Revolted, I stepped back, my stomach churning.

Who in the world would do something like this? I glanced around to see whether anyone was watching. I didn't see anybody.

As I gathered up my courage and stepped up closer again, I could see that blood was still dripping from the rat. Whoever had done this had been here just moments ago!

I started looking around for something to cut the rat loose with when suddenly it screeched and bared its teeth at me.

I jumped back, screaming. That rat wasn't dead!

2

Hysterical, I screamed again. The wounded rat hissed and lunged toward me. It would have sunk its teeth into my flesh except that the string around its neck kept it fastened to the door handle.

I backed away, still screaming.

A man ran out of Luigi's pornography shop next door, yelling, "What's the matter, lady? Somebody try to mug you?"

I tried to answer, but the utter terror of the situation left me speechless. All I could do was point to the rat, screeching and struggling with the string that held him. "Th-th-th-there!" I finally managed.

Sizing up the situation, the man started rummaging in some nearby garbage cans and found a piece of two-by-four that someone had discarded. Then he headed toward the door, where the rat was still screeching and lunging. Every time it lunged, more blood splattered over the door. It was the most hideous, nauseating thing I had ever seen in all my life!

My would-be defender struck the rat, but not hard enough to do anything except make it hiss louder and bare its teeth at him. The man struck again, this time harder. And this time he missed the rat and hit the string. Snap! The string broke, and the rat tumbled to the ground and headed toward its antagonizer.

My defender threw down the stick and took off running as fast as he could go. I stood there, too petrified to do anything. And then that rat turned toward me!

My brain kept sending messages to my feet to move, but I felt as though they were embedded in the cement. The rat, apparently sensing my terror, bared its teeth, ready to attack. And it suddenly occurred to me that this thing could kill me!

The man's stick was out of reach. My only possible weapon was my purse. As the rat headed toward me, I raised my purse above my head, and with all the strength I could muster, I came down on that rat. Splat! It was a direct hit. The rat, weakened from loss of blood, rolled over and kicked a time or two, and then it lay still. I stared, openmouthed, unable to realize what I had just done.

I wasn't taking any chances, so I ran over and got the stick the man had discarded in his hasty retreat. I came down on the body of that rat as hard as I could—over and over and over. By the time I got through, that rat was thoroughly dead. No question.

I dropped the stick, still petrified by what I had just been through. I had never seen anything like this in all my life. Then I looked again at the door of my counseling center, which was all splattered with blood. When I did, I could see that filthy rat hanging there, screeching and hissing and baring its teeth.

That mental image was too much for my stomach. It started churning. My head felt as though it were going in circles. And then I vomited all over the pavement.

An old lady who was passing by noticed the door and me and the vomit and asked, "What happened?"

I tried to answer, but I couldn't. I vomited some more. The stench was enough to gag a person.

I couldn't talk, but I could think. And the big wonder going through my mind was, Why would someone do this to me? Was it because of the gang meeting tonight? Did one of the gang members want to scare me off?

Maybe somebody didn't like the idea of a peace conference.

A crowd started to gather, exclaiming over the rat and the mess. A little kid picked the rat up by the tail as his mother screamed, "Put that filthy thing down! It might be alive!"

But the kid wasn't about to put that rat down. Instead, he whirled it over his head, and people backed up. Then he let it fly, and the rat went sailing across the street.

Just then a woman stepped up to me. "They're after you, young lady," she announced.

I started to ask who "they" were, but by the time I could get the words out, she had wheeled around and was gone. I stood there, nonplussed. What did she mean?

I ran after her, grabbed her, and spun her around. "Ma'am, excuse me, but who is after me?"

She put her hand over her mouth and laughed a hideous, sinister laugh. "They'll get you now!" she blurted out. "They'll get you. They don't spill an animal's blood for nothing. They're going to get you!"

"Who? Who?" I demanded.

She let out another sinister laugh. The chills ran up and down my spine. "Is it the Hidden Skulls or the Tattooed Terrors who are after me?" I asked.

Her eyes grew wide with terror. "The Hidden Skulls? The Hidden Skulls?" she said, trembling. "Oh, no! I have to get out of here!"

She wheeled around and took off running. I almost chased her again, but I decided to let her go. She probably wouldn't tell me anything, anyway.

People were gathered around my counseling center talking about the mess. I decided I'd better go back to the apartment and get Uncle Alex and Aunt Amilda to help me clean it up. We had to do something before the meeting started at seven, and right now I was in no condition to preside over a session to end the war.

When I got back to the apartment, Uncle Alex was sitting at the kitchen table reading his Bible. He looked over his glasses and asked, "How come you're back so soon? Has the meeting been canceled?"

Everything broke loose inside of me. I threw my arms around him and sobbed. "Oh, Uncle Alex," I said, "you'll never believe what I've just been through. When I got to the counseling center I noticed that someone had taken a huge alley rat and splattered its blood all over the door. And then he had tied the rat to the door handle. Only the rat wasn't dead yet, and it started screeching and hissing. A man tried to hit it but only broke the string that held it to the door, and the rat almost got— the rat, the rat . . . the rat. . . ."

By this time I was sobbing so hard I was incoherent. Alex patted my back and said, "Now, Marji, it's all right. Everything's going to be okay. Just settle down."

"Uncle Alex," I wailed, "that rat almost got me! If I hadn't hit it with my purse and stunned it, it would have pulled a chunk out of my leg—maybe even killed me!"

Hearing my cries, Aunt Amilda came rushing in, yelling, "What happened? What happened? Is there a gang war on again?"

Alex recounted what I had just told him. Her mouth flew open. Then she said, "I know what that is. It's the devil trying to stop you from meeting those gang members! The devil knows that if you get those gang members saved, he'll lose a lot of support! Marji, this has got to be the work of the devil. I just know it."

"Aunt Amilda, I know our battle is a spiritual one. I know the devil is against us. But whom do you think the devil is using?"

"I've got several theories," Uncle Alex offered.

"Such as?"

"Well, first, it could be the tactic of some gang members. Just because those two gang presidents have agreed to the meeting doesn't mean they have settled their differences. Maybe one gang is doing this to try to scare off the other gang. Or maybe some member is unhappy because his president has agreed to the meeting, and he's trying to cause trouble."

"I had thought of that possibility," I said.

"Or it could possibly be someone involved in a cult," Alex continued. "There are some crazy things happening down here in the Lower East Side. You know, it could be a satanic cult. They sacrifice animals and sprinkle the blood around, sometimes as a blessing and sometimes as a curse."

"Why would they pick on me?"

"Maybe the girl you won to Christ night before last has a family member who's in one of those cults, and this is his way of trying to intimidate you. Or maybe you've been witnessing to someone who is demon possessed, and the devil is trying to scare you—maybe even scare you out of the Lower East Side."

"Well, that sure terrified me!"

"Marji, Marji," Alex chided. "Remember what you always tell us. You tell us that the power of evil is no match for the power of our Saviour. In fact, I was just reading in the Bible where Jesus said not to be afraid because He is with us. I believe that, Marji. The Lord is with you. He's with Amilda and me. And He's going to be with us in that meeting tonight. We will not allow the devil to get the upper hand. God will help you stop this gang war!"

By the time Alex finished giving me his encouragement, I was feeling a whole lot better. How thankful I was for his sterling testimony. He hadn't been a Christian but a few years. Yet I noticed that the more time he spent reading the Bible and praying, the stronger his faith became. I guess that's what the Bible means when it says that faith comes by hearing, and hearing by the Word of God. It certainly was demonstrated in his experience.

Amilda, aware of how the experience had turned my stomach inside out, said, "Marji, you still look a little pale. Why don't you just wait here, and I'll go down and clean up the door. I'm not afraid."

I must admit my stomach was still quivering. I don't know whether it was that splattered blood or the encounter with the wounded rat. I'll never forget how it looked and sounded. It hissed the way a snake does—almost as though it were the devil himself!

"I'm so mad at the devil," Uncle Alex said to Amilda, "that I'll go down there with you, honey. We'll wipe those doors clean and pray that the power of God will overcome the evil powers around that counseling center. The devil knows he is going to lose some of those precious boys tonight, so he is putting up a really big fight. But the Lord will give us the victory!"

I smiled and relaxed a little. "Uncle Alex, you sound just like a preacher!" I said. "You've encouraged me so much that I'm ready to go take on the devil, too!"

"Hallelujah!" he shouted.

"Praise the Lord!" Amilda echoed.

I couldn't keep still, and we had a wonderful few minutes praising God for the victory we just knew was coming.

Then Amilda grabbed a bucket of water and a couple of rags and said, "Come on! Let's go wash the devil out of that place!"

By this time I was ready for the battle, and the three of us headed for the counseling center. Out in the street, Alex started singing, "This little light of mine, I'm gonna let it shine." Amilda joined in, and then I did, too. We were only three marching down that street, but you would have thought we were an army of at least ten thousand! We were ready to battle the devil!

People who lived nearby and had been converted through my ministry at the center heard us singing and joined us. Then they all started clapping. What a happy, joyous time it was—a time of victory in Jesus!

Amilda led our impromptu parade right up to the door of the counseling center, jammed a rag into the bucket of water, and smacked it hard against the rat's blood, calling out, "Hallelujah! Jesus Christ is Victor!"

People clapped, and Amilda scrubbed. I gritted my teeth as the memories came rolling over me, and once again my stomach started churning.

In spite of all the excitement and seeming air of victory, I couldn't escape the obvious question: Who would do something like this? This evening, when the Hidden Skulls and the Tattooed Terrors met in my center, I'd try to find out if they knew anything about it. But what if they did? Would this become the pretext for more fighting? And if they began fighting in the center, there would be nothing left of it. I was really wondering what I had gotten myself into in arranging this meeting. Oh, well; it was a little late to be worrying about it now. I'd just have to leave it all in the Lord's hands.

Amilda's enthusiasm helped her get the door cleaned up in record time. I unlocked the door, and the three of us went in, along with the other Christians who had joined us. We decided this would be a good time to have a spontaneous prayer meeting.

At about ten minutes to seven we got up from our knees, and I said, "Friends, I believe God is giving us the next hour. When the gang members come in here, let's believe together that some of them—yes, maybe all of them—will get saved. That will end this senseless war."

No sooner were the words out of my mouth than we all heard sirens—lots and lots of them. They seemed to be converging from several directions and kept getting louder and louder and louder.

I glanced through the window and could see several policemen headed our way. Then our door flew open, and more police than I had ever seen in one place came bursting into the center, their guns drawn.

"What are you doing here?" I demanded, horrified.

"Where are all those gang members?" a policeman asked.

Oh, no! This was terrible. All I needed now was to have the police interfere with our meeting tonight. Now those gang members would think I was in cahoots with the police and had arranged the meeting just to get them all arrested!

"Gentlemen, gentlemen. Just a minute please," I said. "There are no gang members here. We are having a church service. We gathered here to pray for gang members."

Would they leave now? But even if I got them out the door in the next minute, would the gang members show up? I knew that none of them would come if the police were anywhere around.

"We just got a report that the Hidden Skulls and the Tattooed Terrors are forming their groups," the police captain said. "We heard they were going to have their rumble here at this counseling center. So, Miss Parker, I suggest that you and your friends get out of here quickly. If they start their gang war, there'll be a lot of blood spilled around here!"

"Gentlemen, we have already prayed," Uncle Alex said. "We believe God. There will be a real fight here tonight, but not between the Hidden Skulls and the Tattooed Terrors. It's a fight between evil and righteousness. It's a battle between Satan and God. But the victory was already settled when Jesus died for our sins at Calvary. So we plan to see a real revival here tonight. These gang members are going to give their hearts to Jesus. They're going to become new creatures in Him."

The captain scratched his head, and a puzzled look creased his face. "Mister," he said, "I don't know much about this Jesus business, but I think you are far from reality. These gangs play for keeps. When they say they are going to have a rumble, they have a rumble. I can't stop them; you can't stop them; nobody can stop them!"

That didn't deter Alex. "God will stop them!" he insisted. "He'll drop them in their tracks. They'll give their hearts to Jesus!"

The captain laughed. "Mister," he said, "you must be a do-gooder who just came to New York City! Have you ever seen a gang war?"

"Officer, I don't want to sound disrespectful," Alex started, "but I've probably been down here longer than you have. I know these people. I've seen the neighborhood run down. I used to be an alcoholic, a real bum. But Jesus came into my life and took away the curse of alcoholism. I've been born again. And my niece here, Marji Parker, has been helping many people. All she uses is the old-fashioned power of God. And it works!"

"Well, I certainly know Marji Parker," the officer said. "I know that some of the girls I used to bust for drug addiction and prostitution are no longer around here. I've heard she's sent them upstate to some girls' home, and their lives have completely changed. I know all about that. But I'm telling you, sir, when you're dealing with gangs, it's a whole new ball game. There's a world of difference between a prostitute and a gang war!"

Alex wasn't about to give up. "No there isn't, sir," he insisted. "Jesus died for the alcoholic like me. He died for the drug addict and prostitute like Patti. And, sir, He died for gang members like the Hidden Skulls and the Tattooed Terrors. Sir, Jesus died to bring them peace!"

The captain laughed again. "I'll tell you what, mister. If the Hidden Skulls and the Tattooed Terrors stop their fighting, I'll become a believer in this Jesus of yours."

Several other officers chuckled. They knew that would have to be a miracle. But I agreed with Alex. It could happen. Jesus could help us stop these gang wars.

"We're going to have to stay here," the captain announced. "We simply can't allow this rumble to take place—it's too dangerous. I hope you don't mind."

"Of course I mind," I responded, a little more testily than I should have. "We've got a message of Christ's love to preach to these gang members. But they sure won't come if you and your men are camped here. Now I can assure you there will be no rumble taking place here tonight. I've talked to the presidents of both gangs, and they have agreed to a truce. They'll be coming to hear the message of Jesus and how He brings peace."

The officers just went ahead and sat down, looking very skeptical about what I had told them. I glanced at my watch. Five minutes till seven. Just five minutes to get those cops out. But how?

"We simply can't let you go through with this meeting, Miss Parker," the captain told me. "I know you mean well, but I don't think you really understand what you're up against. You could be killed."

I stood there helplessly. Then what he had just said really started to sink in. If the gang members did start fighting, some of them probably would get killed. Would that make me responsible for their deaths? After all, I was the one who had arranged this meeting. Were they just using my invitation as an excuse to rumble? That would be horrible. Maybe I'd better go along with what the police captain was saying.

My heart sank. All we had prayed for was coming to nothing. Had God let us down? Had Satan gotten the upper hand? Or had I gotten ahead of God's timing?

Just then Elias Gomez, a twelve-year-old who came to the center quite frequently, rushed in yelling, "The Hidden Skulls are gathered down the street that way. And the Tattooed Terrors are gathered down the street the other way. There's going to be a big rumble!"

All the policemen simultaneously reached for their guns and took off down the street. I had tried to do something to bring peace to this troubled area. Now it looked as though my peace efforts were about to break out into open warfare, with the cops in the middle. Where had I gone wrong?

3

Distraught at the unexpected turn of events, I rushed out of the counseling center onto the street. Quickly sizing up the situation, I realized that some of the cops had run to the right, some to the left. I could make out the gangs, dashing for cover. Then a shot rang out. I couldn't tell where it came from, but I knew what it meant: war!

"Everybody clear the streets!" a policeman yelled.

He didn't have to tell me twice. I dived behind a garbage can as firing, screaming, yelling, and cursing increased in intensity. "Oh, God, forgive me for my presumption," I prayed.

A few yards away, a policeman came out of his hiding place to fire back at a gang member. Suddenly he crumpled. Yelling and screaming, he began rolling over and over right out into the middle of the street!

Up to that moment, I had been thinking about my own safety. Now I faced a dilemma. Should I crawl out there and try to help him? In some way I felt responsible for this whole thing, and I knew I couldn't let him die.

On my hands and knees, I crawled into the filthy gutter. I could hear the bullets whizzing over my head. I had to keep down.

In the distance, I could hear more sirens. The police must have radioed for reinforcements. But would they get here in time to help the wounded officer? I was close enough now to see his pain-wracked face, and I could see he was bleeding profusely.

The bullets were so close now that I got down on my stomach and slithered the rest of the way through that filth to get to his side. By this time, he lay motionless, and I could see blood oozing from a wound in his neck.

I didn't know much about first aid, but I remembered that for an open wound, you should stuff some clean cloth into it and put pressure against it. But where could I find a rag in the middle of a New York City street?

I hadn't worn a sweater. Maybe the officer's shirt would do.

Bullets still whizzed past us, and I knew I'd be taking a chance if I sat up. But I had to do something.

I tried pulling his shirt off, but he was too heavy for me to move around. And the more I jerked at him, trying to get his shirt off, the more he bled. This wasn't going to work.

Where was I to find a cloth? If he lost much more blood, he'd soon be dead.

I glanced down. My blouse! I couldn't take it off out here in the street. But I had to! I gritted my teeth, ripped off my blouse, balled it up, and pushed it hard against the wound. I could only hope it would work. I tried not to think about how embarrassed I felt to be sitting in the street with no blouse on.

I glanced around, but no one seemed to even notice me out there. The police I could see were crouched behind garbage cans, firing. They all seemed to be looking down toward the end of the block. It looked as though the gang members were retreating! Officers started running forward. Then everything went deathly quiet.

Two policemen, crouching low, reached us. One of them looked at the wounded officer and yelled, "They got Conklin!"

Both of them bent over him and started putting

pressure on some of the bigger veins in his neck. One of them glanced at me, and I felt my face get red. But he whispered, "You've got great courage, Miss Parker! Great courage!"

Other officers began running toward us, and in moments I heard the siren of the ambulance. Two attendants jumped out as it rolled to a stop, and quickly put Officer Conklin on a stretcher. One pulled away my blouse and pushed a heavy piece of gauze against the wound. Then he handed my blouse back to me.

The blouse was completely stained with blood. I didn't know what to do. There was no point in putting it on, but I felt so foolish standing there holding it.

The attendants pushed the stretcher into the ambulance. Two officers jumped in back, and the ambulance took off.

I pulled my arms across my chest, trying to cover myself. One of the officers must have noticed me cringing, for he gallantly removed his shirt and gave it to me. As I buttoned it around me, I breathed a little easier.

The police officers regrouped. Apparently Conklin was the only one injured.

I guess the police captain wasn't aware of what had happened, for when he spotted me, he ran over and started to bawl me out. "If this had happened in your counseling center," he started in, "only God knows how many people would have been killed. It's a good thing we got them dispersed—at least for now."

I was still dazed from what seemed like a horrible nightmare. Heavy gunpowder smoke cast an eerie haze over the street. People began looking out of windows and yelling. Amid all that turmoil I knew one thing: I had lost that battle. And I surely would never be able to get the Tattooed Terrors and the Hidden Skulls together again. They'd never trust me after tonight.

The captain kept plying me with questions. How well did I know the Hidden Skulls? How well did I know the

Tattooed Terrors? How many members were in each gang?

I tried to explain that I knew very little about them. I couldn't convince the captain that I felt they really were coming in peace to the meeting. He had made up his mind that they had decided to use my invitation as an excuse for their rumble.

Just then Aunt Amilda came running up with a clean blouse for me. "Marji, I saw you crawl out to that police officer!" she exclaimed. "I prayed that Christ's love and power would protect you out there! And it did!"

I took the blouse from her outstretched hands, excused myself from the captain, and hurried over to the counseling center to change. As I tried to unbutton the policeman's shirt, my hands trembled so badly I could scarcely control them. I guess that was the first time I realized what a close shave I had had. I wondered how many guardian angels it had taken to protect me!

When I finally got my clean blouse on and returned to the street, I quickly located the policeman who had lent me his shirt, and handed it back to him. "Thanks," I told him. "You are a real gentleman."

He smiled. "Miss Parker, you don't know me," he said. "I'm Officer Gatim and I'm a Christian."

"Officer Gatim, I was about the most embarrassed I've ever been in my life when I was out there. Thank you for doing something about my problem."

"It was the least I could do," he responded. "You've done a very courageous thing. You probably saved Officer Conklin's life!"

"I guess I really didn't stop and think about what I was doing," I said. "I saw him out there, so I just crawled out and did what I could."

"Let me tell you," he said, "your act will never be forgotten by the department."

The captain came back and started in again. "Now, Miss Parker, you've just got to leave those gang members alone. They are mean, ornery, and unpredictable. They care very little about anyone but themselves. They don't care about policemen, and they don't care about you. They were just using you. You saw what happened here tonight. Those thugs will shoot at anything!"

I knew the captain was right, humanly speaking. But I also knew that Jesus cared about what happened to those gang members. And if He cared, then I would care, too. And He'd help me find some way of reaching them.

As the police began filtering away to other duties, Alex, Amilda, and I headed back to the counseling center. Some other Christians joined us for another prayer meeting. I sensed that some of us—including me—felt kind of licked.

But not Amilda. "This isn't defeat," she told us. "This isn't a setback. God knows what He's doing. I believe the Lord will give us another chance at those gang members. I know it!"

I didn't feel like saying amen. I felt humiliated and drained. I had had one big chance, and I had blown it. Would I ever have another?

But we all prayed for a while. Then I locked up the center, and the three of us headed back to our apartment. Amilda made coffee, and we had some of her home-baked peanut butter cookies as we sat around and talked and analyzed and figured and what-iffed.

When I finally went to bed, my mind was still going in circles, and sleep just wouldn't come. I couldn't sort everything out—starting with the horrid rat and the blood all over the door of my counseling center. Was it voodoo? Black magic? A warning from the Hidden Skulls to Ratface, head of the Tattooed Terrors?

I rolled and tossed, glancing at the clock every few minutes. At 2:20 A.M. I told myself I just had to get to sleep. I'd slip my mind into neutral. . . .

Suddenly I became aware of someone pounding incessantly at our apartment door. I jumped out of bed, slipped into my robe, and headed for the door, wondering who it could possibly be.

At the door, I looked through the peephole. I couldn't believe it. There stood Benny Barnes, the pimp.

What did he want, at this hour of the night? Numerous times in the past, he had threatened to kill me because I had talked to his girls—his prostitutes—and had gotten them saved and sent them up to the Walter Hoving Home. But Benny seemed to have forgiven me for that when we went through that kidnapping plot. He had saved my life, and I saved his.

"What do you want, Benny?" I called.

"It's a life-and-death matter, Marji! Let me in!"

Should I? Was it some kind of a trick?

He pounded again. "Please, Marji, believe me! Please! Please! I need your help desperately!"

Uncle Alex came running out as I started undoing the latches. Maybe my prayers were being answered. Maybe God had gotten Benny under such conviction that he had come to find out how to be saved!

When I got the last bolt undone and started to open the door, Benny pushed his way in. He looked terrified, and was completely out of breath. "Marji, come with me. I need your help!"

"Not so fast," I responded. "What happened?"

"Four of my girls are in deep trouble. If something doesn't happen right away, they're going to get killed!"

"Has some pervert got them?" Uncle Alex asked. "Are you planning to use Marji as a decoy?"

"No, nothing like that, Mr. Parker," Benny said. "But I need Marji to come with me. This situation is bad news. I mean, I can't handle it alone. I have to have Marji with me!"

"Why do you need Marji?" Aunt Amilda wondered out loud.

I was glad she asked, for that was puzzling me, too. What problem was so desperate that Benny needed me at half-past two in the morning?

"I can't tell you," Benny answered. "All I can say is that you have to trust me. I need Marji, and I promise I'll bring her right back."

Trust Benny? A shiver ran down my spine. How far could I trust any pimp? If I knew Benny, he had something up his sleeve. These pimps would do anything to make money.

Uncle Alex wasn't fooled, either. "Benny, I understand you're the most successful pimp in town. Even though you've lost a few of your girls to Jesus, you're not going to get by with any trick like this. So why don't you just walk out that door and forget about us. It just won't work."

Benny stomped in anger. "Mr. Parker, for crying out loud, listen to me, will you? I tell you I'm just going to use Marji. I'm not going to do her in. I'm just going to use her, but I can't tell you why. Can't you trust me?"

"Benny," Alex said, "I don't trust the devil, and I don't trust a pimp. Excuse me for being so harsh, but that's the way it is. I've been around too long. I know how you guys operate. No way is Marji going to leave here with you tonight."

Benny wrung his hands in frustration. "Please!" he begged. "I thought you folks were Christians and that Christians helped people in trouble. I need help, and I need it desperately."

"Benny, we know you need help," Amilda said. "What you really need is Jesus in your life. You need to give up that horrible life-style of yours and surrender your life to the Lord. Now if you'll just sit down over there, we can share with you from God's Word how you can be set free. I'll put some coffee on, and. . . ."

Benny turned toward the door, burying his head in his hands. "I just hate to do this to you people," he said.

"Marji, I've come to appreciate and respect you. And I respect you, Mr. Parker. So this is something I hate to do. But you leave me no choice!"

He reached into his coat pocket, wheeled around, and there he stood, with his gun pointed at Alex. "Sorry, folks," he said, "but this is the way it has to be."

Then, pointing the gun toward me, he added, "Okay, Marji, you're coming with me."

Looking down the barrel of a gun, I knew I had no choice.

"Benny Barnes, you'll never get away with this!" Aunt Amilda yelled. "God has His hand on Marji's life. If anything happens to her, you'll be held responsible. God will punish you severely, I can promise you that!"

"Now, now, Mrs. Parker. Don't get mad at me," Benny soothed. "This is something that I just have to do. I have no choice."

"Okay, Benny, it looks as though I have to go with you," I said. "But first, tell me what's so urgent."

"I'm in a jam; I mean, a real jam."

"What kind of a jam, Benny?"

"Okay, I'll tell you. But whatever you do, don't try to stop me!"

I looked over at Alex and Amilda. They seemed as puzzled as I was.

Benny stuttered, trying to find the right words. Then he blurted out, "You have to promise that after I tell you what's happening, you won't call the cops or anything like that. If we blow this thing, people are going to get killed. And Marji, you might get killed, too, if your aunt or uncle calls the cops!"

Benny sure was painting a dark picture.

"You three people know what happened this evening," Benny started. "The Hidden Skulls and the Tattooed Terrors were ready to kill. I mean, ready to kill."

"I sure know that," I interjected. "In fact, they almost killed a policeman."

"Marji, you don't get it. That's not what I'm talking about. When both gangs were marching to your counseling center, they were coming to make peace. Then all of a sudden, they saw those cops rushing out of there. When they saw that, they were thinking only of one thing."

"What do you mean by that?" I asked. "I suppose you mean that they were thinking about killing a few cops."

"That's what you think!" Benny responded. "They were thinking about you!"

"Thinking about me? That's strange."

"Don't you get it yet?" Benny asked in surprise. "They thought they had been set up. And they thought that you, Marji, were the one who set them up!"

"What?" I yelled. "Did I hear you right?"

"You heard me right. They think that you, under the guise of religion, planned that setup and had those cops planted there so that when the two gangs arrived, the cops would be able to bust them! Marji, they are so mad at you that they have a death warrant out for you!"

I gasped. Amilda's hand went over her mouth as she reacted in horror. Even Alex furrowed his brow deeply.

"Benny, you know I wouldn't do a thing like that. Uncle Alex and Aunt Amilda can confirm it. In fact, we were there having a prayer meeting, praying for a real miracle, when those policemen came bursting in. I had nothing to do with their being there. I even tried to get them to leave. I told them the gang members would never come as long as they were there. I wouldn't set those boys up."

"I believe you, Marji, but they don't. And that's the problem."

I stared at Benny unbelievingly. Then I wondered why he was involved in this. What was he doing here at this hour? And he had said he was in danger. They didn't think that Benny had brought the police there, did they? And what was I going to do? If they had a death warrant out on me, I couldn't walk the streets anymore. Was God trying to tell me I needed to get out of the Lower East Side for a while?

"Now here's the situation, Marji," Benny went on. "When all the shooting started, I was a few blocks away with four of my girls. Then I saw the Tattooed Terrors running down the street. The next thing I knew, about seventy-five of them had surrounded us. They grabbed me and spun me around. They pulled zip guns; they pulled switchblades; they said it was all over for me."

"But Benny, you had nothing to do with it. Absolutely nothing!"

"That's what I tried to tell them. But they knew I tried to save your life once, and I guess they figured I was involved in some way. Well, they grabbed four of my girls and me, and they forced us to go with them to their headquarters in the basement of one of those burned-out old tenement houses.

"The president of the gang said he knew you," Benny went on. "And he knew that I knew you. So do you know what he's demanding? Marji, you won't believe this!"

Without waiting for me to answer, he went on: "Marji, they have demanded that I bring you alive to their headquarters. They want to talk to you."

"Benny, you know it would be suicide for me to go there now," I said. "Those guys have hot tempers. They're vicious. I'd rather wait a few days until they've cooled off and I can reason with them."

Benny raised his gun. "That's not the way it's going to be, Marji," he said with an air of finality. "Those guys have four of my best girls. They said that if I don't bring you tonight, they're going to kill them. Then they're going to find me and kill me. And then, Marji, they're coming to get you. They're going to kill you, too. So you have to come."

"What?" I asked in shock. "Are you telling me the truth, Benny?"

"Marji, for crying out loud. I'm not lying. I may be a mean old pimp, but I'm not a lying pimp. Those bums have my girls, and they'll kill them. You have to come with me!"

"Benny," Uncle Alex said, "you've got to understand about these gangs. You can't trust them. Do you really think they'd believe Marji if she talked to them? They've probably killed your girls already. And they'll kill you and Marji if you go back there."

"Mr. Parker, if they've already killed my girls, I'll take this gun and blast those dudes to smithereens!" Benny exploded. "I mean, there's going to be blood and guts all over the place. I'll kill every one of those Tattooed Terrors myself. You can count on that for sure."

"We don't need any more bloodshed," I said calmly. "Benny, I'll go with you. But so help me, if this is some kind of a trap or a trick, don't forget that God is watching. You'll have to answer to Him, not to us."

"I'll go with you," Uncle Alex volunteered.

"No, we can't have that," Benny quickly interjected. "The Tattooed Terrors made me promise to bring only Marji. And no cops. You'd better believe that when we walk into the basement of that tenement, there will be gang members up on the roofs, across the alley, and down the street. If we're being followed, they'll kill us without batting an eyelash. So please, Mr. Parker, whatever you do, don't try to follow us, and don't call the cops!"

Uncle Alex, realizing the gravity of the situation, shook his head. "You've got my word, Benny. I won't call the police."

Benny tucked his gun inside his belt. I hurried into my bedroom and quickly changed. When I came out, Aunt Amilda had Benny sitting at the kitchen table. She was telling him he needed to know Jesus as his Saviour. I sure hoped it was sinking in. This pimp had caused me no end of grief since I'd been in the Lower East Side.

Benny and I walked down the completely deserted street for four blocks. Benny didn't say one word. That scared me because he usually was so talkative.

At East Sixth Street, we turned a corner and walked two more blocks. I was scared to death to be on the streets at this hour, and suddenly wondered why Benny hadn't driven his Cadillac.

In the middle of the block were several burned-out tenements. Was one of these the headquarters? The moonlight made the scene so spooky and scary that my heart was beating like crazy.

As Benny directed me into one tenement, I glanced across the street. Silhouetted in the moonlight were the shadows of four men, holding rifles trained in our direction. I felt as though I was going to faint. How could I possibly escape death by going right into the headquarters of the Tattooed Terrors?

4

When Benny noticed me stagger slightly, he grabbed me and pleaded, "Come on, Marji. Don't pass out on me now. In a few minutes this should all be over with."

All over with? Maybe that was prophetic! Maybe in a few minutes my life on this earth would be ended with a blast from a Tattooed Terror's rifle!

"I guess maybe I felt faint because we were walking so fast," I explained. "How come you didn't drive?"

Benny clenched his fist. "Those bums took my new Cadillac, too. I mean, that car is very precious to me. I paid a bundle for it, and I sure want to get it back."

We walked down some filthy stairs, through an underground passageway, and then came to an open area where garbage and filth was strewn everywhere.

I squinted, and could just barely make out four gang members guarding a door. One of them grunted, "Over here."

As we got next to them, I could see that all four of them had their shirts off. Across their chests were hideous tattoos. One was especially so. It showed a snarling devil with horns and a pitchfork. But the devil's face was like that of a rat. It reminded me of the rat that someone had strung onto the door of my counseling center.

The gang members motioned us through an open door, and we stepped through into another hallway. My knees were knocking together as I wondered whether there was any way we could make it out alive.

Two gang members led the way down the hall. The other two followed us. They sure weren't taking any chances.

They stopped at a door and knocked in some sort of code. Then one of them hissed, just like a rat.

The door opened, and we stepped into a room dimly lighted by a few candles. A pall of sweet smoke hung over everything. I smelled marijuana. Immediately, we were surrounded by the whole gang. I remember thinking that Benny's estimate of seventy-five must be pretty close. There was certainly no getting out right now. They all had zip guns or switchblades, and their weapons were very much in evidence.

Their leader, Ratface, stepped forward. I recognized him from the tattoos I had seen on his face the other night. But he had his shirt off now, revealing hideous tattoos across his chest. His eyes spit out hate.

"Okay, Ratface, I brought her to you," Benny said. "Now give me my girls, and I'll split."

"Not so fast, Benny," Ratface responded. "We have to wait a few minutes to be sure this isn't another setup." Then he turned toward me and spit out the words, "This filthy, dirty dog here knows all about setups, don't you, preacher lady?"

"Now wait a—"

I hadn't even finished my sentence before he took another step toward me, brandished his switchblade, and ordered, "Shut up!"

We waited, no one saying a word. My hands felt clammy. My knees kept knocking, and my heart was beating so fast I could hardly think.

When Ratface seemed sure that no police had followed us, he started in: "All right, preacher lady, why did you set us up? I agreed to come to that meeting as a personal favor to you because of what you did to help my mother out and because you scared off the junkie who was trying to get me. Now don't go thinking any big ideas, like I owe you something because you saved my life. I'd have gotten away from that turkey as soon as I hit the streets. My boys would have seen what was going on. You just made it happen a little faster, that's all. Anyway, I was coming to that meeting as a favor, and then you took advantage of us and called the cops in. Preacher lady, we don't forgive things like that. We've been talking about it while we were waiting for you to come. We decided we're going to cut you up in little pieces and feed you to the rats. That's what we do to people who betray us!"

"Now wait a minute!" I said it more forcefully than I felt. "I did not set you up. All I wanted to do was to get a peace conference going between you and the Hidden Skulls, and—"

The words *Hidden Skulls* started the whole group hissing. Some bared their teeth at me.

"Okay, everybody cool it!" Ratface ordered.

He certainly seemed to have total control over this gang, for with just that one order, they all immediately quieted. But they still stood there with guns and knives.

"Come on, Ratface," Benny pleaded. "I've upheld my part of the bargain. I've brought her. I didn't call the cops. Now give me my four girls and my car and let me out of here."

That dirty Benny! He was planning to leave me there all by myself. Now I knew I'd never get out of there alive.

Ratface turned to one of the gang members and ordered. "Garbage, get the girls."

Garbage ran into another room and reappeared with the four girls, all of whom appeared to have been badly treated.

"What have you done to my girls?" Benny wailed.

"We had to teach them a lesson," Ratface said curtly. "One of them tried to break out of here, so my boys beat up all four of them. You're lucky they're still alive. The boys wanted to finish them off."

I stared at those four poor, frightened girls. They looked as though someone had pummeled them mercilessly. I guess they were lucky to still be alive.

Ratface shoved the girls toward Benny. "Take them!" he ordered.

As soon as he did, two gang members stepped forward and grabbed my arms. "You're not going anywhere, preacher lady," one of them warned. "One false move, and it's all over for you!"

I stood there, rigid. No way was I going to try anything. Believe me, I was praying for God to deliver me from this evil. But all that came to mind was how John the Baptist was beheaded for his witness. His head ended up on a platter. Would mine be offered to vicious rats? I shuddered.

While the two gang members held me tightly, Benny and his four girls headed for the door—and freedom.

When they were gone, Ratface said to me, "You know, we ought to kill you. I lost one of my boys in that battle with the cops. We ought to take your life for his."

What could I say? *Oh, God,* I prayed silently. *Give me the words to change this situation.*

In a flash, I thought about what I had once read in the book *The Cross and the Switchblade.* It told of the Reverend David Wilkerson's encounter with Nicky Cruz, a notorious gang member. Why shouldn't I say the same thing in this situation?

"Ratface," I started in, "do you know something? Jesus loves you, and I love you, too."

The whole gang became hysterical, screaming and hissing.

"Don't give me any of that religious bunk!" Ratface exploded. "We have all kinds of religious do-gooders down here on the Lower East Side, but we gang members have to fight to stay alive. So don't tell me anything about Jesus or anybody loving me because I simply don't believe it!"

Undaunted, I blurted it out again: "But Jesus loves you!"

Whap! Ratface had stepped forward and backhanded my face. I recoiled. Then I remembered: that was exactly what Nicky Cruz had done to David Wilkerson. Was God working in the same way here?

I remembered something else David Wilkerson had told Nicky, so I said, "Ratface, you said you were going to cut me up in little pieces. Well, if you do, every little piece is going to love you."

The gang members really started to hoot at that one. Some of the girls—the debs and dolls—pointed their fingers at me and yelled, "Hey, preacher lady, do you really know how to love? Really love? How many guys have you been with?"

My face flushed, but I turned toward one of those girls, pointed my finger at her, and demanded, "What's your name?"

Surprised and, I guess, chagrined, she stepped back a pace or two. I repeated, "What's your name?"

"Bedrock."

"Bedrock," I said, "Jesus is going to make a great Christian out of you!"

I really don't know why I said that. It just came out. But the whole gang thought the idea was hilarious, and they began to taunt Bedrock. One of them yelled, "You have to give up your evil ways, Bedrock!"

They all laughed, but Bedrock didn't. God's Spirit had struck an arrow into her spirit, convicting her of her sin.

I whirled around and pointed at Ratface. "God is telling me right now, Ratface, something about you. There's someone in your family who is a Christian and has been praying for you. Right?"

The sneer on his face suddenly disappeared. He stared at the floor, wondering how I could possibly know that.

I couldn't. But God was working a miracle by the power of His Holy Spirit. He was revealing things to me about these gang members, and using that information to convict them of their sins!

I pointed at him again. "Ratface, answer me. Who's been praying for you?"

He looked at me sheepishly. "My grandma," he replied, and then shifted his gaze to the floor again.

As soon as Ratface admitted that, I noticed that the other gang members started backing away from me. Even the two who had been holding me let go. They didn't want me to tell things about them! Great peace surged over me, driving out fear. God was working!

I pointed toward a huge fellow who was standing near the back of the group and said, "Young man, what's your name?"

He started backing away until he was up against the wall.

Somebody yelled out, "Tarzan, kill her! Tear her limb from limb!"

He looked as though he could do it. But right now God was directing me to tell him something.

Unafraid of what he would do, I walked over next to him and looked up into his face. He must have been every bit of seven feet tall, and muscular. But I pointed my finger right up at his face and said, "Tarzan, God tells me that you were a Christian once. You're a backslider, aren't you?"

His mouth dropped open. Gang members standing nearby stirred uneasily. They were waiting for him to tear me apart.

But Tarzan just turned his head, afraid to look me in the eye.

"Tarzan, God tells me you were once born again. You were filled with God's Holy Spirit, but you've now fallen into deep sin and ended up in this gang. You've tried to act tough. You've tried to kill. But behind all this, you're scared to death. God's been talking to you, Tarzan, and you know it. You know that if you had died in that shoot-out tonight, you would have gone to hell. Isn't that right?"

He kept avoiding my eyes. So I reached up, grabbed his chin, and forced him to look at me. Gang members gasped. They had never seen anyone mess with Tarzan! But it wasn't really me. I could feel God's Spirit directing me every step of the way.

Forcing Tarzan to look at me, I said again, "Tarzan, your days are numbered. You'd better get right with God."

He threw his arms out wide, let out a bloodcurdling scream, and dropped into a heap on the floor, weeping and wailing.

Over across the room, I heard two of the debs and dolls begin to scream. There must be others here who had once known the Saviour. The ghetto has a lot of the Gospel. People who hear the message start to walk with Jesus, but give up when the pressure gets too great.

I went over to one of the girls who was screaming, put my hand on her forehead, and said firmly, "I rebuke this spirit in the name of Jesus. God, set this girl free!"

She fell to her knees, sobbing. God was working in her life.

I noticed all the gang members edging against the wall. They knew something was going on here—something that couldn't be explained in human terms. They were seeing God at work!

Full of God's Spirit, I turned around to find Ratface. He was the one I wanted to get. He was the one they all respected and obeyed. Get the leader, and you get the gang!

But I couldn't see him anywhere. Where had he disappeared to?

As I walked about that room, gang members stepped back whenever I got close to them. I noticed something else: the switchblades and zip guns were no longer in evidence. And no one laid a finger on me as I moved freely about that room.

"Where's Ratface?" I demanded.

Everybody stared at me, but no one answered. I asked it again.

Just then, I heard a bloodcurdling scream come from a nearby room. It sounded worse than Tarzan's yell! Then a door flew open, and there stood Ratface, with two huge rats underneath his arms. He held them firmly by the backs of their necks as they hissed and kicked, straining to get free.

The gang members began to scream excitedly. "Let the rats kill!" one of them yelled.

Ratface lunged toward me, and the rats hissed and bared their teeth. "Marji Parker, you'd better say your prayers," Ratface said mockingly. "In a minute, I'm turning these rats loose on you, and they'll eat the flesh off your bones!"

A couple of the girls screamed in terror. I stood there, trembling. What was I going to do now?

Then I remembered how God had shut the lions' mouths when Daniel was cast into the den of lions for praying to God. But that was a long, long time ago. Would God shut these angry rats' mouths and protect me?

Ratface set the two rats on the floor, still holding them by the scruff of their necks. They were hissing and straining to get at him. One of them almost got his leg! These had to be the meanest rats I had ever seen.

"These rats haven't been fed for five days," Ratface yelled. "They're used to human flesh, and they're ready to devour some right now!"

All the other gang members were backing up. Most of them had pushed themselves clear up against the wall. It seemed evident that these rats hadn't been trained to attack only enemies; they would get whatever was in their way. It was useless for me to think of running, so I just stood my ground, praying fervently for God to intervene. I had just witnessed God performing miracles in this place, and I sensed that this was an attempt of the devil to stop it.

"Marji Parker, you deserve what you're about to get," Ratface hissed. "You set us up with those cops. Now we're going to avenge the blood of our brother. These rats will tear the flesh from your body bit by bit and eat you alive!"

Suddenly I knew who had hung that filthy rat on the front door of my counseling center. It must have been some members of this gang. Maybe they wanted to scare the Hidden Skulls. Maybe they wanted to scare me. But obviously, the rats were an important part of their gang ritual.

"Get ready, Marji Parker!"

As calmly as I could I said, "Ratface, you know what you're saying isn't the truth. My only reason for calling you two gangs together was to tell you about Jesus. He loves you and wants to change all your lives. You won't find real living in fighting and killing. Real life is found in Jesus! He'll give you the peace you're searching for. He's here with us right now. If all of you surrender your lives to Him, the war will be over. The battle of life—the battle you thought you'd lost—will have been won by you. You'll have won it in Christ!"

"May the blood of our brother be avenged now!" Ratface shrieked as he let loose one of the rats.

It hissed and bared its teeth as it started toward me. I stood my ground. It was going to have to be up to God whether or not that filthy rat sunk its teeth into my flesh. If I became a martyr, it was God's will.

I gritted my teeth and shut my eyes tightly. I heard the

rat hiss, but I felt nothing.

Then, across the room, I heard gang members screaming. I opened my eyes and saw that rat, clear across the room, chasing one of the girls! Oh, she was screaming in absolute terror! But the rat was gaining. Suddenly it leaped, sinking its teeth into her leg. Blood spurted, as the poor girl literally tried to crawl up the wall! Then a shot rang out, and the rat rolled over, dead.

"Scarface, you killed my best rat!" Ratface screamed hysterically. "You killed him! You killed him!"

"But Ratface, I couldn't let him kill my girl," Scarface yelled back. "I couldn't let him do that!"

Ratface still held the other rat. I called to him, "Don't let that rat loose. God is here. You have seen His judgment. If you let that other rat loose toward me, only God knows what is going to happen. I'm warning you, in the name of the Lord!"

"Ha!" Ratface sneered. "You don't scare me with any of that religious talk." He jerked the other rat up off the floor and headed toward me, holding the rat up near my face.

"I ought to let him eat out your eyeballs first!" he screamed. "And then your nose and the rest of your pretty face. Then who'd come to hear all your talk?" He roared a hideous laugh.

I blurted out, "Turn that rat loose on me if you want, Ratface. Even if I end up looking like the most hideous person on the face of this earth, there's one thing you'll never drown out. You'll never drown out the voice of God within my soul. Till my last dying breath I will tell God's message throughout the world. I will tell it in the Lower East Side. I'll tell it in the tenements. And I'll tell it right to your face. Ratface, Jesus died for your sins. He loves you. He wants to rip out all that hate and bitterness that you have within you, and replace it with His love. So no matter what happens to me, Ratface, that's my message. If you want to turn that rat loose, turn it loose. But no matter what happens to me, Jesus loves you!"

I sounded brave, but when I looked right into the face of that huge, filthy rat, I felt my knees buckle. Was I going to faint? How would Ratface react to that? Would it remind him of how I had saved his life and helped his mother?

He stepped back a few paces, bent over, and put the rat on the floor, facing it toward me. Suddenly he gave it a shove in my direction and started yelling, "Kill! Kill! Kill! Kill!"

The other gang members tried to melt into the wall. Even Ratface moved back a few paces.

Once again, I stood firm. The Lord had deterred the other rat and protected me. Would He do it with this one?

Right then, my mind went to Stephen, the first Christian martyr, who was stoned to death for his faith in Jesus. God hadn't chosen to deliver him from death. Why should I expect. . . .

I kept my eyes open this time and saw that rat, hissing and screaming, lunge toward me. Then it seemed as though it hit some kind of an invisible shield. It stopped cold in its tracks and looked almost perplexed. It crouched, ready to spring forward again. I stared down at it and said firmly, "In the name of Jesus, I command you to shut your mouth!"

The rat hissed and lunged again. But it couldn't get past what I guessed was an invisible barrier God had put there to protect me!

"Kill! Kill! Kill! Kill!" Ratface's screams still echoed through that room.

The rat kept on hissing. Then the rest of the gang began to chant: "Kill! Kill! Kill! Kill! Kill!"

I pointed at the rat again and said, "In the name of Jesus, stop!"

It was almost as if I had shot that rat. It jumped high in the air, somersaulted, and lunged right at Ratface!

That so caught Ratface by surprise that he simply stood there, screaming in terror. Now the rat was tearing at his legs, and Ratface was begging, "Help! Help! Somebody help!"

The gang members weren't about to get involved with that rat. They scattered to get as far away as possible. Ratface tried to run, too, but he tripped on some old boards and fell. Immediately, that rat was all over Ratface, snarling, hissing, screaming, biting.

Ratface screamed again: "Somebody please help! Somebody help!" But his gang brothers just kept backing away.

Suddenly I was aware that the rat was going for the jugular vein! It surely did know how to kill! Any minute now, it would be all over!

I stood there, petrified. I couldn't let that rat devour Ratface. But what could I do? Was he about to die the same way he had made other people die?

He tried to push the rat away as he begged, "Somebody help me! Please!"

I had no gun, no knife. This time I didn't even have my purse. The only thing I had to fight that rat with was my foot. Maybe I could catch it by surprise, since it was concentrating on Ratface.

I ran over and kicked as hard as I could. My toe caught the rat right in the stomach, and the rat went sailing across the room until it smacked hard against the wall and crumpled to the floor. It shuddered a time or two, and then lay still.

Ratface was still rolling and tossing on the floor in terror. I knelt beside him and held him close. "Ratface, it's okay now. The rat is gone. You're safe."

He stared at me in disbelief. I repeated, "You're safe, Ratface. Look over there, against the wall."

He rolled over and looked where I was pointing. He

still couldn't quite understand all that had happened.

I slowly got to my feet as the gang members gathered around, all trying to talk at once. Still on his back on the floor, Ratface raised his hand to silence them. Then he screamed at them, "Why didn't any of you help me? Why didn't you help me?"

"I was going to help you," Tarzan said. "Believe me, I was going to do it."

Ratface rolled over and slowly stood up. Every move he made was painful, but he tried to ignore his wounds. He looked the gang over and then spit out in disgust, "Just when I needed you most, you all let me down!"

None of them would even look him in the eye, and he stood there, defeated and dejected.

Finally, he turned toward me. "Marji Parker, I don't know why you did it, but you saved my life again. If that rat had severed my jugular vein, it would have been all over for me. I owe my life to you."

"Ratface, it really wasn't me," I explained. "I didn't have the power to kick that rat over against the wall and kill it. God is the One who saved your life. You owe your life to Him! Isn't that right, Tarzan?"

Tarzan broke out in a grin as big as his face. "That's right, Miss Parker," he said. "God has been here tonight, and He's been performing great miracles!"

I threw my arms around Ratface's shoulders and said, "God's not through with you yet, friend. He's spared your life for a purpose. And let me tell you, that purpose is something good!"

The rest of the gang members clapped and cheered. They knew I was on their side. And I knew that God was going to do something special for this gang. Maybe this was His way of stopping the war!

I was about to explain the plan of salvation when suddenly the door burst open and what seemed to be a whole army of policemen rushed in. Right in the middle of them was Captain Wiley, and he was shouting, "Everybody freeze!"

Ratface's jaw dropped open as he stared at me in disbelief. I knew what he was thinking: I had set him up again. For a moment there, he had softened in his attitude. Now all that hate was back on his face, and he looked as though he could kill me without provocation.

Why did the police keep showing up at the wrong moment?

5

"Okay, everybody up against the wall!" Captain Wiley ordered.

I could see gang members' fingers twitching. Would they go for their switchblades and zip guns? A fight in these close quarters would be a real bloodbath!

The captain must have sensed what I did, for he yelled, "Don't anybody try anything funny, or it's death for four of your brothers!"

He nodded, and four police marched in behind four gang members, their guns to the boys' heads. They must have been the four snipers who had been out on the roof. The police had taken them by surprise!

"Everybody up against the wall, and get your hands up!" Captain Wiley ordered again. Nobody moved.

"I'm counting to three. If you don't do as I say, my men will start shooting. Now move!"

The four officers holding their guns at the gang members' heads tensed. I couldn't let this happen. But what was I going to do?

"One."

The hatred and rebellion were so thick in that room you could feel them. Those gang members weren't going to move!

"Two." Were they calling the captain's bluff? The tenseness cut through the air. Was I about to witness that bloodbath?

Just then Ratface, muttering, turned and headed for

the wall. When he broke, the other members quickly followed his lead. I guess he had some respect from his brothers.

"That's more like it!" Captain Wiley yelled. "Now get those hands up high!"

Officers moved in and started to frisk the members. All the guns and switchblades they pulled off those boys constituted quite an arsenal. The police knew they could at least get them for possession of illegal weapons.

Now the police started flipping out handcuffs. I tensed as a cop went toward Ratface. Would he submit to this?

As the officer grabbed Ratface's arms and spun him around, the gang leader screamed at me, "Marji Parker, I'll kill you for this! You almost had me believing all that religion bit. But now you've done this. I know what you were doing before—you were stalling!"

I ran over to him and said, "Ratface, that just isn't true. I had absolutely nothing to do with the police coming here. What I said to you a few minutes ago, I still mean with all my heart. Jesus loves you, and I love you, and don't you ever forget it!"

Ratface sneered at me. I turned, but not fast enough. He spit in my face!

The officer roughly spun him around, clamped the cuffs on him, and shouted, "That's no way to treat a lady, much less a preacher lady! I ought to kill you!"

"It's all right, officer," I said, wiping off my face. "He really doesn't know what he's doing."

The cop laughed derisively. "He doesn't know what he's doing? He's the meanest gang president in this city—maybe in the country."

Ratface looked straight at me and snarled, "Someday I'll get out of the slammer, and I'll get you, Marji Parker. When I get out, I'll kill you!"

Then a voice behind me boomed, "Hey, man, cut that lip before I blast your tongue out of your mouth!"

I wheeled around, wondering what officer would be

talking that way. That's when I spotted him: Benny Barnes!

"Benny, what in the world are you doing here?" I asked, almost in shock.

"Hey, Marji, I'm not that stupid," he answered. "When I got out of here with my girls, I knew exactly what was going to happen. I've heard about this gang and their hungry rats. Well, I just couldn't let that happen, so I went to the police."

"Really? You went to the police? Well, I never would have—"

"Don't rub it in. There has to be a first time for everything. Besides, I couldn't stand a little twerp like Ratface pulling something on me. And when I got to my car, they'd already stripped it. I mean, nobody is going to get by with that!"

I was about to ask Benny if his car was more important than I was, but Captain Wiley yelled, "Okay, everybody outside. Now! We have to book you little rats!"

His sarcasm wasn't lost on me, but I was still concerned about my relationship with Ratface and the rest of the gang. Would they ever believe that I had nothing to do with calling the police?

As the officer pushed Ratface by me, I said, "Don't forget. You may think you're coming to look for me, but I'm going to be looking for you. I'll never give up until you surrender your life to Jesus!"

"Ha!" Ratface snarled. "I'll never surrender. And now there's two people I'm going to be after when I get out: you and that miserable pimp Benny Barnes. No way will that big dude get by with bringing the cops in here! He's in for big trouble, now. There's going to be one dead pimp as soon as I get out!"

That was too much for Benny, and *pow*! He came down hard with his fist right in the middle of Ratface's jaw. That spun him around, causing him to lose his balance and tumble to the floor. As quickly as a cat, Benny was on him, pummeling him.

All the other gang members started screaming and hissing and trying to get into the action. A big policeman put a gun to Benny's head, yelling, "Get off him, Barnes. He needs to be killed, but we can't do it while he's got handcuffs on!"

Benny reluctantly rose, still steaming. "Ratface, you'd better never step outside that jail," he threatened, "because as soon as your foot hits that sidewalk, your flesh will be blasted all over the buildings! There won't be enough left of you for a funeral when I get through with you!"

Ratface was fuming, too, but the officer pulled him off the floor and pushed him out the door before the two could scuffle again. As he went out the door, Ratface turned and spit in my direction again. I was too far away for it to hit me. But it painted a graphic picture of his total disdain for me and for what I was trying to do. Would I ever again have a chance to reach this gang?

I knew all the gang members would be booked and probably jailed for a while. But I also knew that eventually they would get out. And then it wouldn't be safe for me to walk the streets of the Lower East Side.

It was quiet and spooky in that room, now that the gang members and the police had gone outside. Benny came over. I knew he had intended well, so I started to thank him.

"You don't owe me any favors for what I did," he said shyly. "You saved four of my girls, so I saved you. That means we're even."

With that, he turned and headed for the street, and I followed him. I noticed again what a big, handsome guy he really was. I knew he was mean—he had a reputation of beating his girls if they didn't bring in enough money. And yet I couldn't help but remember that an ornery guy like Saul became Saint Paul the apostle. If Benny would just surrender his life to Jesus, what a tremendous witness God could make out of him! I sure was praying for that!

"I still don't have my car," Benny said as we got to the street. "You'd better let me walk you to your apartment. I got you into this mess tonight, and I want to see you safely home. Okay?"

I was more than happy to accept that offer.

As we walked, Benny said, "Marji, you're really quite a girl. You've more spunk than any woman I've ever known. I sure can't see why you bury yourself in that counseling center. Why don't you come work with me and make some real money?"

"Benny," I answered, "you just don't understand yet, do you? I'm a Christian. Christian young ladies simply don't get involved in prostitution."

"You don't understand, either," he replied. "This is not prostitution. This is just performing a service. A lot of businessmen come to town and want a little fun, and they're willing to pay for it. So my girls provide it. There's nothing the matter with that, is there?"

"Are you kidding? What you call 'fun,' God calls 'sin.' The Bible says it's adultery and fornication."

Benny laughed. "There you go with that Bible business again. Marji, you're an educated woman. You know that the Bible is just a collection of stories. Oh, they're nice stories; but you don't really believe them, do you?"

I stopped and shook my finger at him. "If you only knew, Benny. God has some wonderful promises in the Bible for us, and I believe them. In times of adversity and in the problems we face in life, we can stand on God's promises. He comes through every time."

He laughed again. "I suppose now you're going to tell me that God rescued you tonight. Well, listen here, Marji. You might as well get your feet on the earth again. It wasn't God who called those cops; it was Benny Barnes, the mean old pimp, who called them."

"Benny, I appreciate what you did. But there's something else you don't understand. God uses people to work out His purposes and will. You have never gone to the cops before, have you? Why did you go tonight? Because God put it in your heart to do it. It wasn't God's will for me to die down there in the headquarters of the Tattooed Terrors, so God used you to save me."

"Nice try, Marji, but I can't believe that. This old world is hell—it's all the hell we'll ever see."

"I know this world is a tough place for a lot of people, Benny, but there is a literal heaven and a literal hell. And God wants you to go to heaven, Benny—He really does!"

I then told him about how God had protected me from the rats. He didn't respond at all. I knew God's Spirit was speaking to him, convicting him of his sins. And I sensed that this wasn't the time to press the issue. So we walked on in silence, each of us with our own thoughts.

About two blocks from my apartment, as we were crossing a street, we noticed a car bearing down on us. I screamed, and we both jumped back onto the curb. It screeched to a stop right next to us and the driver jumped out, his gun drawn.

"Hold it right there, Benny!" he screamed. "I've been looking for you all night. Now one false move, and it's all over!"

I'd never seen this dude before. I ruled out "cop." I noticed his car was big, and looked expensive. And apparently he knew Benny.

Benny instantly obeyed the order. So did I.

The man moved closer until his gun was right under Benny's nose. "Okay, what did you do with Cecelia?"

Oh, oh! These pimps sometimes steal girls from each other. They have what they call "stables," or groups of girls they use for prostitution. Evidently, Benny had stolen a girl from this other guy, who sure fit the description of a pimp.

"Come on, Cobra," Benny said. "I didn't steal her. She told me she didn't want to work for you anymore. She came over to me voluntarily."

Cobra's left hand slapped Benny's face. "That's a dirty lie, and you know it. Cecelia would never leave me. I mean, never!"

"Cobra, now you listen to me!" Benny ordered. "Cecelia came to me all bloody and bruised from a beating you had given her. She told me she just couldn't take it from you any longer."

"Hey, are you trying to lecture me about beating a few women? I know all about you. You beat your stable up all the time! And you know that's the truth!"

When Cobra yelled, "I'm going to blast your brains out!" I figured I'd better step back, before these two started something.

"Hey, cool it, will you?" Benny said. "I didn't mean any harm. Okay, so I did talk to Cecelia. I mean, I couldn't help it if she really wanted to work for me. But you know I'll give her back to you. So just put that gun down."

"You're not going to get by that easily!" Cobra exploded. "You're going to give me my Cecelia, and you're going to do it right now! Get in my car! We're going to go get her."

With his gun, Cobra motioned Benny toward the car, telling him to get into the backseat. As soon as Benny was situated, Cobra said, "Okay, hand me your rod, nice and easy."

As Benny reached into his pocket, Cobra yelled, "Not so fast! I'll take care of that rod."

When Benny handed him the gun, Cobra tucked it under his own belt. Then he reached into his pocket and

flipped out a pair of handcuffs. Was this guy a policeman?

"Okay, Benny give me your hands!"

"What?" Benny yelled. "You wouldn't do that to me,
would you, man?"

Cobra sneered, "I just want to make sure you're kept
safe and sound. You know I wouldn't want anything to
happen to you! Besides, I'm not about to drive you anywhere with you sitting loose!"

Benny stuck his hands under him, so Cobra waved the
gun right in his face. "Listen, man, I'm not joking. Give
me both hands!"

"Hey, I'll go with you," Benny protested, "but please,
no handcuffs. I mean, I flip out whenever someone puts
handcuffs on me. Please, no handcuffs. I won't try anything."

Cobra cocked the gun. "Listen, man, I don't care
whether you flip or not. We're not going anywhere until
I get these cuffs on you. Now give me both hands!"

Benny reluctantly stuck out his hands, and Cobra
snapped the cuffs on one hand. He reached behind the
seat and snapped the other one onto a post of some kind.
Poor Benny had to sit in a rather twisted position.

Cobra slammed the door and started to move around
to the driver's side. It was just two blocks to my apartment, and I hoped I could make it okay. I could call the
authorities from there and tell them about Benny's being
abducted.

I had taken only a couple of steps when Cobra yelled,
"Stop right there, lady! I said, stop!"

I stopped.

"Turn around, slowly."

I did that. He had his gun pointed right at me. "Where
do you think you're going, anyway? Nobody walks out
on Cobra. Now get over here and get in this car!"

"Listen, Cobra," I protested, "you're reading this all

wrong. I don't belong to Benny. I'm a Christian young lady who—"

His laugh interrupted me. Then he said, "I suppose you're going to tell me you're a nun who's out here preaching."

"I wouldn't make fun of nuns," I said, irritated. "They're good people, and they help—"

Once again his raucous laughter interrupted me. "You girls all make the same kind of excuses, don't you? I've had girls tell me they were senators' wives or they were preachers' wives. One even claimed she was the daughter of the president! So listen, kid: get smart, before I blast your pretty face off!"

Well, I sure didn't want to get into that car and be taken by Cobra to who knows where—but I had a good idea for what purpose! So with a "I am no prostitute," I turned and started toward my apartment. I heard a gunshot. Nothing happened, so I kept walking. Then I heard footsteps running behind me. Cobra grabbed my hair and jerked it, spinning me around. As he did, he slapped me hard across the face, screaming, "No woman has ever run away from me and gotten by with it! Not even you! Now get in that car before I really mess up that face. And if you mutter as much as one word, I'll kill you right there. That's one way I can get back at that Benny. He's got my Cecelia, and now I've got one of his girls. So any trouble out of you, and I'll drop you in your tracks!"

I started to protest that I wasn't Benny's girl, but Cobra slapped me across the face again, screaming, "Not one word! Not one word!"

To emphasize his point and get me moving, he threw his arm around my neck and squeezed until I could scarcely breathe. Then he started dragging me toward his car.

The more I tried to resist, the harder he squeezed my neck. And he still had that gun out. It could accidentally go off and kill me! So I decided resistance was foolish.

Cobra pushed me into the backseat with Benny, yelling, "Not a word out of either one of you. Not one word!"

As I fell into the backseat, I looked over at Benny pleadingly. He had a funny look on his face—almost like a smile! But I was furious! Why hadn't he told Cobra I wasn't his girl? There was no way I was going to be a prostitute for either of these pimps!

Cobra got in, started the engine, and must have floored the accelerator. Tires screeched as we took off.

"Now, Benny, let's go get Cecelia. Where is she?"

"Down on Delancey just off Bowery Street."

"Man, you'd better be telling the truth! If you're not, it'll be the end of you and your girl!"

On Delancey Street, we pulled to the curb, where two prostitutes were leaning against a nearby building. "Who are those girls?" Cobra asked.

Benny tried to lean forward for a better look, but he was held fast in a very uncomfortable position. "They're not mine," he said.

Cobra spun around. "Listen, Benny, I never did trust you. Now where's my Cecelia? You'd better produce her right now!"

"Cobra, cool it, will you?" Benny replied angrily. "I mean, this is where I had her tonight. Maybe she's with a customer. Now let's just hold on a few minutes."

We waited, Cobra drumming his fingers on the seat impatiently, glancing this way and that. I began to pray. Whoever this Cecelia was, she had better show up soon, or there was no telling what this Cobra would do to Benny and me!

Finally Cobra eased out of the car, saying, "I'm going to have a look around."

When Cobra was out of earshot, Benny whispered, "Marji, I'm sorry I got you involved in this. As soon as that Cobra gets out of sight, take off running as fast as you can. This dude is meaner than I am. I mean, he's killed several people!"

"But what about you, Benny? What will he do with you?"

"Don't you worry about me. I'll figure out something. But it's better if one of us gets away. That'll distract him and might make it easier for me to get away. Now as soon as I tell you, you split. Go somewhere and call a cab home."

We both watched as Cobra walked a few feet away, pacing back and forth. Then he started toward the corner, his back to us. I grabbed the door handle. Every muscle in my body tensed.

Benny, watching intently, suddenly whispered, "Now!"

I jerked the door handle. Nothing happened. I jerked again. Still nothing! Locked!

I reached to unlock it, trying to pull the knob up. It wouldn't budge! "It's no use, Benny—we're locked in!"

"Jump over the front seat and get out. That door won't be locked."

I scrambled over the front seat, grabbed the handle on the driver's door, and jerked. The door opened! But as I slid out, Cobra spotted me and came racing back. "Hey, what's going on here?" he demanded.

What could I tell him? I couldn't lie! God wouldn't honor that.

"I was trying to escape," I responded matter-of-factly.

Cobra laughed. "Of course you were trying to escape. I knew that. That's why I didn't go far away. Couldn't get out the back door, huh?"

I nodded.

"You're absolutely stupid," he said. "If I had wanted to, I could really have done you in."

"Yes, I guess you could have," I answered. "You could have shot me before, too."

"No, nothing like that. You're too cute to shoot. I just

wish you were working for me. You look fresh and beautiful. I could make two hundred bucks every time you were with a trick. I mean, baby, you and I could do great in this business!"

When I didn't respond, he said, "Here, let me show you something."

He flicked a switch under the dashboard and said, "Now touch the door handle."

I did. I don't know how much juice there was in that handle, but it almost knocked me silly. I jerked back and screamed.

Cobra laughed. "I was going to set that switch when I got out, but I decided not to. Sometimes that electrical shock can almost paralyze people. I had it installed so that when I put my girls in the car, they know better than to try to get out!"

I wasn't amused, and I was getting more and more frightened as Cobra forced me back inside the car. While he had the back door open, he yelled at Benny, "I'll give you five more minutes. If Cecelia doesn't show by that time, I'm taking you to the river. I'll blast your brains out and throw you in."

"For crying out loud," Benny responded, "I can't make her appear out of thin air. I'm no magician. Maybe she got busted! But, as I said, she's probably with a trick. Just be patient."

"Don't you give me orders!" Cobra snapped back. "We've already been here half an hour. That's plenty of time. I think you're stalling!"

I looked over at Benny and pleaded, "Come on, tell Cobra the truth. I've got to get home."

"Marji, keep your mouth shut!" Benny screamed. "I know what I'm doing!"

I thought I'd better cool it. I sure couldn't afford to make Benny mad.

The next five minutes seemed like an eternity. I kept praying that Cecelia would show. Benny kept staring at the floor. Did he have some plan up his sleeve?

Cobra held his wrist up, staring at his watch, and counting out those last ten seconds. ". . . four, three, two, one! Okay, Benny. Your time's up! I warned you, and now you're going to get it!"

He revved up the engine, and we took off in the direction of the East River.

Would he really kill Benny because of this girl? And what was going to happen to me? I had a suspicion he wouldn't kill me, but he might have in mind for me a fate that, in some ways, could be worse than death!

6

Cobra drove wildly to Thirty-fourth Street, where we pulled into an alley and stopped behind a warehouse along the East River. Benny was trembling. Did he know this was the end?

"Listen, Cobra, I'll make a deal with you," he said. "I mean, I have a great deal."

"Sure, you have a deal now," Cobra sneered. "Especially when in a few minutes you'll end up at the bottom of that cold, filthy river where all the fish can eat you!"

"Listen, Cobra. Now listen to me," Benny pleaded. "I can make you a terrific deal."

"You'd better start talking fast," Cobra answered. "In two minutes, it will all be over for you."

"Okay, here's the deal," Benny said. "This girl with me tonight is my best girl. I mean, she makes all kinds of money for me. Just look at her. Fresh, clean—she's got everything. She's the kind the big spenders really go for. And she's a real workhorse. So here's my deal. I'll sell her to you for one thousand bucks. Now I could easily get twenty times that much. But you can have her for a thousand if you let me go free. Is it a deal?"

"Why should I pay you a thousand bucks?" Cobra responded. "What I ought to do is just kill you and take the girl for free."

"Cobra!" Benny screamed. "Come on! I mean, you wouldn't do anything like that, would you?"

As if in answer to Benny's question, Cobra pulled out

his gun and put it to Benny's head. Was I about to witness a gangland-style execution? Poor Benny! He had no way to defend himself.

"Cobra!" Benny screamed. "Please, please don't! I'll make it five hundred bucks. Let me go, and you can have her for five hundred bucks. I promise she'll make you thousands and thousands of dollars. I'm rich, filthy rich, because of Marji Parker."

"That's a lie!" I yelled. "A dirty lie!"

Both of them laughed. Cobra pushed his gun back under his belt. Then he pulled out a wad of bills, peeled off five hundred dollars, and tucked it into Benny's pocket.

"Okay, it's a deal, man, but she'd better produce, or she knows what's going to happen to her!" He looked at me menacingly.

I couldn't believe this was really happening. I was being sold, just like a slave, into a filthy, disgusting profession! I pinched myself, hoping I would awaken to realize it was a horrible nightmare.

Cobra quickly unlocked Benny's handcuffs. I figured while he was occupied with that, I'd better cut out. But as I tried to scoot out the door, Benny grabbed my arm. Then I heard two clicks. Now I was handcuffed!

"You just stay put, Marji Parker," Cobra ordered. "You're mine now, baby. And you'd better produce, or I'll kill you! Do you understand?"

I stared angrily at Benny. Why would he do something like this to me—was it just to save his own skin?

When I looked at him, he started laughing. "Come on, Marji. Just settle down," he said. "I know you'd rather be with me than with Cobra, but a deal's a deal. Think of it this way: You saved my skin. So just relax, and you'll live happily ever after!"

"Oooh, you!" I started. Several pretty strong curse words came into my mind. I hadn't used words like those since before I was converted in college. But it had been a long time since I was this angry. I bit my tongue to keep from saying them.

"Now, now, Marji. Be a nice little girl," Benny soothed. "Everything will turn out all right."

He patted my hand, pushed himself out of the car, and started to walk away.

"Benny, you come back here and straighten this thing out!" I yelled. He just turned around and waved at me. Oh, I was furious!

Cobra pushed me back into the backseat, slammed the door, and we took off. He drove along Thirty-fourth Street and then turned up Eighth Avenue, heading toward Times Square—the worst area of the city!

Let me tell you, I prayed like I had never prayed before—even harder than when I faced those rats. Then I had felt like a martyr standing true to God. Now I simply felt used and frustrated. Why would God let something like this happen to me?

When we got to Fortieth Street, Cobra turned toward the Avenue of the Americas. Everything seemed dark and deserted as we pulled over to the curb.

Cobra got out, opened the back door, and said, "Okay, Marji, are you going to cooperate? Or will I have to teach you a few lessons?"

I stared at him defiantly. Then I screamed, "I will never, never, never do this. I am not a prostitute! I am a Christian!"

Whap! Cobra slapped my face hard. I recoiled, but there was no way I could defend myself with my hands handcuffed behind me.

"I had a suspicion you were going to be tough to deal with," Cobra said. "But baby, I have my ways."

"Well, I've got my values!" I responded. "I have very high moral standards!"

Whap! "Listen, girl, don't get smart with me! No woman has ever talked back to me and gotten by with it! I've slapped a few of them around. I've broken arms;

I've broken legs; I've even broken a few heads. Now I paid five hundred bucks for you, and I'm going to get that money back with interest tonight. So you'd better cooperate, or it's back to the East River, where you're going to end up as fish food!"

It's strange, the twists your mind takes when you're in a stressful situation. All of a sudden, I remembered Aunt Amilda and Uncle Alex, home in the apartment waiting for me. They must be beside themselves by this time. For all they knew, I was still in the headquarters of the Tattooed Terrors. They probably worried that the gang members had killed me. I wondered whether they were still afraid to call the police. Alex had given Benny his word that he wouldn't. How I wished I could at least call and tell them that I was still alive.

When I snapped back to reality, I realized I was still staring at this menacing pimp who thought he owned me. I wasn't about to submit to any man willingly. So what was he going to do?

It didn't take me long to find out. He whipped out his handkerchief, wrapped it around my head and over my mouth, and tied it tightly. When I squirmed, he slugged me as hard as he could in my stomach. I doubled over in unbelievable pain.

He pushed me onto the floor of the car and commanded, "Stay down there! Don't you even think about getting up until I tell you!"

I tried to mumble something, but no words could come out. The gag even made it difficult to breathe, it was so tight.

Cobra got back up in front and took off again. This time I had no idea where we were going because I couldn't see out the window. But finally he parked again, and I could recognize where we were—in front of the Hilton Hotel.

Without any explanation, Cobra left the car. He was probably looking for a customer for me. Just the thought of it tied my stomach in knots. I felt as though I was going to vomit, but I knew I couldn't let that happen. I'd choke to death, with the gag in my mouth.

After what seemed like an eternity, the back door opened, and a man got in. He bent over me, staring as he examined me.

"Yeah," he finally said, "you're right. She is a cute little thing, isn't she?"

I tried to scream that I was a Christian; I was no prostitute. But I couldn't force any words out.

Cobra got in, and we took off again. "Okay, mister," he called back, "the price is two hundred dollars."

"What? I've never paid that kind of money for a girl in this town!"

"Now wait a minute!" Cobra cautioned. "We agreed in the lobby that you'd pay me two hundred dollars. I told you I'd get you the best for that."

I was stretched out on the floor of the backseat staring up at the man. My hands were still handcuffed behind me, and I was gagged. Talk about feeling helpless. I knew there was no way I could successfully fend off his advances.

"Okay," the man said, "she looks good. Here's your money." He pulled out a wad of bills, peeled some off, and handed them forward. Then he looked down at me and smiled. I tried screaming, but only mumbles came out.

He patted my cheek, and I begin to kick. "Hey, you've got a little tiger back here," he called to Cobra.

Cobra laughed. "Well, that's what you wanted, didn't you?"

The man laughed and started pulling at my blouse. Then he started to jump on me. When he did that, I kicked again—and this time I landed a good blow. He leaped off, screaming. "That hurt, woman! I mean, that really hurt! Now stop it!"

Cobra bellowed, "What's the matter, mister? I

thought you were a cowboy from Texas who could tame wild horses."

"This isn't funny," the man responded. "This one is really tough. I think we'd better get a room somewhere."

"Okay, but that'll cost you twenty bucks more."

"Okay. Nothing's going to happen here in this back-seat. It'll have to be in a room."

"I know of a hotel on West Forty-eighth," Cobra said. "I think we can get a room there without any hassle. There's hardly anyone around this time of night."

So far, I had successfully fought this monster off in the car. But would I succeed in a room? How could I possibly be a match for both of them? Once again, I felt nauseated.

When we stopped, I realized we were in a run-down area of the city, where a lot of sleazy hotels were located.

"I'll be right back," Cobra said as he rushed off. In a few minutes he came back, opened the rear door of the car, and announced, "Okay, I made a deal. Give me the twenty bucks."

The man unquestioningly peeled off a twenty and handed it to him. Then Cobra leaned over me. "Okay, Marji, you'd better cooperate with this gentleman, or I'm going to throw you off the roof of this place. They'll find you splattered all over this pavement!"

What a choice! If I yielded, could I ever go through with something so absolutely disgusting? But if I resisted, would I be killed? Maybe I really didn't even have a choice! If Cobra held me, there would be absolutely no way I could protect my honor!

Cobra grabbed me underneath my arms and jerked me out of the car. I glanced around, hoping for some kind of deliverance. But there wasn't a soul in sight except the three of us.

The hotel was as I expected: dirty and run-down, a

real fleabag. The room couldn't have cost more than ten dollars.

Why wasn't there a cop around anywhere? It certainly would arouse his suspicion to see someone handcuffed and gagged being led into a hotel. Maybe an upright citizen would see us and call the police. But the streets were totally deserted.

Cobra pushed me into the lobby and nodded knowingly to the clerk on duty, who looked at me and guffawed. "Cobra, you certainly bring in some strange characters! But this is the first time I've seen you bring in one in handcuffs! Is she a real tiger?"

Cobra nodded again. "Charley, you know how it is when you're breaking in these wild ones. Sometimes you don't get much cooperation. But I'm sure this one will soon settle down. And if you mind your own business, Charley, I might even arrange for you to get something free now and then!"

Charley rubbed his hands together in gleeful anticipation. I shuddered. I couldn't, in my wildest imagination, think of having to be in bed with a creepy, crumby character like Charley!

Cobra pushed me up the stairs to the second floor, down a hallway, and into a dirty little room. The man slammed the door behind us as Cobra pushed me onto the bed.

"Okay, you hold her down while I do the business," the man said.

With that, he started to unbutton his pants. I squinched my eyes; I didn't have to watch this rape. I tightened every muscle in my body. I would resist with everything that was in me!

Then the phone rang. I looked up in time to see the two of them exchanging worried glances.

"I'd better get it," Cobra said. "Charley might want to tell us something we need to know."

He picked up the phone and listened for a few seconds. Then he slammed it down, yelling, "The cops are coming! That was Charley! He said they're on their way up!"

I have never seen two guys move so fast in all my life. They almost knocked each other out, both trying to get out the door at the same time! Cobra got out first. Then I heard them running down the hall, probably to the fire escape. They surely wouldn't go down the way we came up!

I lay there half laughing, half crying. The police were coming! God had indeed delivered me from a fate worse than death!

Finally I heard a noise out in the hall. It must be the police! I tried to yell so they would know where I was, but I couldn't make any noise through that gag. I had to let them know where I was, or those two turkeys would be right back as soon as the police were gone.

I worked myself off the bed and ran toward the still-open door. I kicked it open all the way, and looked right into the face of Benny Barnes!

I tried to push him aside because I knew I had to escape from him, too. He had sold me into prostitution, and he wouldn't hesitate to take me back to Cobra. In fact, that would probably earn him a reward!

As I pushed by, Benny said, "Marji, don't run! I'm on your side!"

I tried to wriggle away from his grasp, so he grabbed me with both hands and pushed me up against the wall. "Marji, Marji. Calm down! I'm your friend!"

I kept on squirming, motioning toward the stairs. "Marji, there are no cops coming," he said calmly. "I'm the cop." With that, he reached into his pocket and pulled out a police badge.

When he finally jerked Cobra's handkerchief off my face, I managed, "Benny, what in the world are you doing here? I thought—"

He quickly told me to be quiet, that Cobra might be just down the hall and could hear us. Then he pushed me toward the exit.

As we walked he said quietly. "Marji, can't you trust me? My selling you was all part of my plan for getting us away from Cobra. I knew that if I got free, my chances of getting you free would be a lot better. You didn't like me to sell you for five hundred dollars?"

"Most certainly not!" I sputtered. "And you really did have me scared."

"Marji," Benny laughed, "I'm your friend. I wouldn't sell you for five hundred bucks. Maybe for ten thousand, though."

I didn't think that was funny, either.

"As soon as Cobra took off from down there by the river, I got a cab and tailed you," Benny explained. "It took time because of all those stops he made. I knew I'd have to take him by surprise, and I didn't think I could do that while he was in the car. Then I saw him head over here. That's when I decided to do my cop routine. I always carry a badge—just in case."

"But how did you do it?"

"Well, right after you started up the steps, I pulled the badge on that guy at the desk." We were walking through the lobby about then, and Benny nodded at Charley, calling out, "I got me one!" He pushed me toward the front door, continuing his story. "When I pulled that badge, the guy's eyes bugged out. He thought he was being busted. But I just asked him which room they were taking you to. I told him I wouldn't bust him for prostitution if he cooperated. So he immediately told me. I explained to him that I mostly wanted to catch the girl—that it would be okay with me if he called the room and told the guys the cops were coming."

"Pretty sharp," I said. "You knew you couldn't pull the cop routine in the room."

"Right. I waited in the hall until those two guys were

down the fire escape. No telling where they are, now."

By this time we were outside, and I took a deep breath. It felt good to breathe freely, even if the air wasn't country fresh!

"Okay," Benny said, "let's try one more time to get you home. We can worry about these handcuffs when we get there. The main thing right now is to get out of this area. Cobra can't be very far away."

"Benny, I've heard about fellows taking the long way home with their girls, but this is getting ridiculous. I think I'd be safer to try it on my own."

We both giggled, but we both knew it was out of the question. How could I possibly get home with handcuffs on? Talk about being easy prey for muggers, rapists, or whoever happened to be on the streets at this unearthly hour.

Benny noticed Cobra's beautiful car still parked there. "No sense in taking a taxi when we can ride in style," he said. "Besides, I need a new car. Those Tattooed Terrors finished off mine."

He grabbed the door handle, but immediately he shrieked and jerked back. "That thing is loaded with electricity!" he shouted.

We hurriedly moved down the block, but when we turned a corner, we ran smack into Cobra. The minute he saw us, he whipped out his gun and pointed it in our direction.

"Well, well, what have we here?" he asked. "I thought you sold Marji to me, Benny. What gives?"

"Well, as a matter of fact, Cobra, we've been looking for you," Benny lied. "You see, Marji's got these hand-cuffs on, and she needs someone to take them off. Could we borrow your key?"

Wow! Benny sure was being bold!

"Benny, you must be insane!" Cobra snarled. "I ought to unload this gun right in your belly!"

"Hey, Cobra, come off it," Benny said. "Of course she still belongs to you. I know that. The reason I want you to let her loose is that one of her regulars would like to use her. You know what I mean, man?"

"What are you getting at, Benny?"

"Well, just minutes ago I was heading toward a hotel where a couple of my gals were working. I had this guy with me. All of a sudden he remembered Marji and insisted she was the only one he wanted. Would you believe I told him to wait, and then I went looking for her? And I found her like this, wandering around in the street out in front of that old hotel up the block!"

"That's a dirty lie, and you know it, Benny Barnes. You really must think I'm stupid."

I knew Benny was stalling. Was he hoping, as I was, that a police car would drive by? My eyes searched the streets. Nothing seemed to be stirring.

"Okay, Cobra, call me a liar if you want to," Benny said. "I'll show you who the guy is."

"You'd better be able to produce him," Cobra warned. "If he is there, I'm going to get the money he pays for being with Marji. And if he's not there, I'll kill you!"

"Come on," Benny responded. "I'll show him to you."

With that, he led us back to the hotel where Cobra had taken me. Benny pointed toward it. "Marji, that guy is sitting in the lobby in there," he said. "You'll recognize him. Tell him I sent you."

"Wait a minute!" Cobra protested. "The cops are in that hotel. We just ran out of there to avoid them. No way am I going to go back in there!"

"Oh, come on, Cobra," Benny said reassuringly. "If the cops were in there, they're gone by now. I don't see any cop cars in the street. But that guy is in there waiting for Marji, and he's got lots of money. You might even get your whole five hundred bucks back at one shot!"

The mention of money was too much for Cobra. "Well, okay. But I sure hope this isn't a setup. The guy wasn't a cop, was he?"

"Oh, for crying out loud, Cobra. Don't you think I've been around long enough to tell an undercover cop? Everything is going to be all right. You're going to make a lot of money—I might even make a little. Now come on; let's get this over with."

Benny explained that Cobra would have to take off my handcuffs first. Then he could follow the two of us to the hotel, keeping his gun trained on us to be sure we didn't try anything.

"When we get into the lobby," Benny said, "you'll see the guy sitting there. I mean, this is on the level."

I knew what was about to happen. We had just come through that lobby, and the only person in it was Charley. When Cobra discovered that Benny had duped him again, I just knew he would start shooting.

"This had better be on the level, Benny, or it's all over for you!" Cobra warned.

"It's on the level," Benny insisted. "Now let's get going by getting those handcuffs off. This guy won't stand for handcuffs."

Cobra pushed his gun into his belt and reached into his pocket for the key to the handcuffs. That's when I saw Benny's fist fly through the air, landing solidly on Cobra's jaw. Cobra reeled, and Benny gave him a hard shove, grabbing his gun as he did. Cobra ended up flat on the pavement, rubbing his chin in obvious pain. Benny stood over him, aiming the gun right at Cobra's heart.

"I hate to do this to you, Cobra," Benny said, "but this whole thing has gone too far. This Marji is no prostitute. She never has been, and she never will be. It's a shame the way you've treated her tonight. What I ought to do is pull the trigger of your gun and send you into eternity right now!"

"No! No!" Cobra pleaded. "Benny, have mercy on me! I'm your friend, man. You wouldn't kill your friend!"

"Some friend!" Benny sneered. "If Marji wasn't standing here, I'd do you in right now. I'm sick and tired of you. You're trash!"

Cobra was squirming all over the pavement. "Stop right there!" Benny ordered. "Don't try anything foolish!"

The key to the handcuffs had tumbled to the street in the altercation. You can be sure I had kept my eyes on it. I pointed it out to Benny and he went over, picked it up, and unlocked me—all the while keeping Cobra covered.

He grabbed the handcuffs and told Cobra to roll over and keep his hands behind his back. Cobra was too terrified not to obey, and *click!* Now the tables were really turned. Cobra was held by his own handcuffs!

Benny jerked him to his feet and, pushing him toward his car, demanded, "Tell me how to get that electricity turned off."

"Take the key out of my pocket," Cobra said. "The end of the key is plastic. As soon as you push it in and unlock the door, the electricity shuts off automatically."

Benny had the gun to Cobra's head as he pulled out the key. He pushed it into the lock and turned it. I heard something click. Then Benny grabbed one of Cobra's hands and mashed it against the door handle. I guess he figured if Cobra wasn't telling the truth, he'd get the electrical charge. But nothing happened.

"Now get out of my sight quickly, before I change my mind and shoot you!" Benny ordered.

He didn't have to tell Cobra twice. He took off running as fast as he could, still handcuffed. And Benny still had the key. Well, one thing was certain: I was free. Benny was going to take me home in Cobra's car. I knew those two would be able to settle their differences later. All I really cared about right then was getting home. I was so physically and emotionally drained that I was about to drop.

Benny was still holding the gun when a police car rounded the corner and headed in our direction, flashing its spotlight on us. The light reflected off Benny's gun, and he grabbed me and started shaking me. Now what was up?

7

While the police car stopped and two cops got out and headed our way, Benny kept shaking me. Then he started hollering, "Okay, lady, you can stop your preaching at me. I've heard enough of that stupid stuff!"

I looked at him in shock as he shook me again and screamed, "You're not going to convert me, you religious nut!"

I tried to push away, but he held me close and whispered, "Quick, grab my gun. Slip it under your waistband. I'm dead if they catch me with a rod."

I felt something push against my stomach. "Don't look down, stupid," he whispered.

Before I could respond, I felt him pull my waistband out and push the gun inside. Then he shoved me away from him.

"Hey, what's going on here?" one policeman called as he walked up to us.

"Listen, officer, I don't know who this gal is," Benny started. "She just walked up to me and started preaching at me. I've got my business, and I guess she's got her business. But I don't like people messing in my business. Do you understand?"

I backed away, feeling very conscious of that gun. Was it making a bulge? Would the police notice it?

"Hey, aren't you Benny Barnes?" the officer asked.

"Sure am. And, may I ask, who are you?"

"Don't you remember me, Benny? I busted you once

down on the Lower East Side—on Houston Street."

Benny jumped back. "Man, I forgot all about that. You haven't come to bust me again, have you? I've been living straight since then!"

The cop looked over and seemed to be staring right at my waistband. Did he suspect something? I knew why Benny wanted to put the weight on me. But if the police searched me and found the gun, would I be the one to go to the slammer? I had to get rid of that gun. But how?

"Hey cop, your charge didn't stick," Benny told him.

With that, the policeman grabbed Benny, spun him around, and pushed him against the wall. "No," he yelled, "but I've got you this time! Don't try to tell me you've gone straight! I know better!"

"Hey, wait a minute!" Benny protested. "You've got nothing on me!"

"That's what you think!" the officer replied. "We've been watching you. We saw you bringing the gal to the hotel. We're busting you for solicitation."

Benny squirmed, trying to turn around, but the policeman took his nightstick and pushed it against his head, yelling, "Just stay cool, man, or I'll wrap this stick around your neck!"

The cop looked over at me and asked, "Do you know this dude?"

"Yes, sir. He is Benny Barnes."

"Do you know anything about him?"

I knew I had to be truthful. "Yes, sir."

"What?"

"Well, sir, I know he's a pimp."

The policeman laughed. "Lady, you didn't tell me anything we both didn't know!"

While one cop held Benny, the other frisked him. My heart was beating like crazy. Would I be next?

Should I tell them about the gun now? Something held me back. After all, this was the second time tonight Benny had saved my life. I did owe him a little something for that. For a fleeting second, I contemplated pulling the gun and holding the cops at bay while Benny escaped. Then I could explain. But I realized that was a ridiculous idea. I could be arrested for interfering with an officer. Besides, I really had no idea how to use a gun. And pulling a gun on police officers in the line of duty—I sure couldn't rationalize that as the Christian thing to do!

Sure enough, one of the cops walked over to me. "What was Benny Barnes saying to you when we walked up?" he demanded. "Was he trying to get you to work as a prostitute?"

I laughed nervously. "No. I'm trying to get Benny Barnes to work for me."

The policeman drew back in surprise. "Do you mean to tell us you operate a house of prostitution and want to use Benny Barnes to procure for you? That guy is pretty good at rounding up girls, that's for sure. You might have a prosperous business with old Benny."

"You two have it all wrong," I said. "I'm in a business that lasts for eternity."

Even the officer who was still holding Benny against the wall raised his eyebrows on that one. I wanted to blurt out that I was trying to win Benny to Christ. But would this be the right time to say that?

The patrolman took a step toward me and, pointing at my stomach, asked, "What's that?"

The other cop had loosened his grip a little on Benny by this time, and he turned his head to see what his partner was pointing at.

"Officer," Benny called, "that young lady is pregnant. Now don't get so personal."

Just like Benny—always lying, cheating, conniving. If somehow I could get that guy converted, he could turn all that energy and ingenuity into something useful!

The policeman ignored him and asked again, "What's that?"

I knew better than to lie. I opened my mouth to start to explain when Benny cut in with, "You lay a hand on her, cop, and I'm going to be the one busting you. You know you're not authorized to body search a girl. You know that's against the law. Right?"

The cop backed off. "He's right, ma'am; I can't search you. But I think this is the only time he's ever been right."

Benny laughed heartily over his victory. The cop who was guarding him slammed him up against the wall again and quickly slapped handcuffs on him. Then he spun him around and started pushing him toward the patrol car.

"Hey, man, where are you taking me?" Benny demanded.

"In!" the policeman replied. "I don't know yet what I'm going to book you for, but I'm going to book you—maybe for sassing an officer—maybe for solicitation for prostitution—maybe for bank robbery. I don't know yet, but I'll come up with something!"

Benny struggled so hard that the other officer grabbed him, too. "We have him for resisting arrest," one of them said, and they pushed him into the backseat of the patrol car.

Puffing and angry, one of the cops turned toward me and said, "Okay, let's get this straight. I'm not out here on this street at this hour for my health. I know Benny Barnes. He's one of the meanest dudes in town."

He didn't have to tell me Benny was mean; I knew that. He had tried to kill me a couple of years ago. But I also knew he had stuck his own neck out twice tonight to save my life.

"Officer, I don't want to be rude," I said, "but Benny Barnes isn't all bad."

"You little smart aleck!" the officer exploded. "You're brainwashed, just like all the other prostitutes. You think that living with a filthy pimp is utopia. And you're nothing but a dirty slave. He won't let you think. He won't give you an inch of freedom. All you can do is sell your body and then take the money and lay it at your master's feet. All you dirty prostitutes and your pimps ought to be run out of town!"

My heart went out to that frustrated cop. I knew his job was no picnic. And he described to a T what life was like for the prostitutes of this city. I couldn't understand, either, why they stayed with their filthy pimps.

But you should have seen the startled look on that cop's face when I announced, "I'm a Christian."

He jumped back, threw up his hands, and roared, "Well, if that doesn't beat all. I've been on the beat for years, but this is the first time I've met a Christian prostitute. I suppose next you'll tell me that you pray so you can find guys to solicit and so the cops won't arrest you!"

I smiled at his sarcasm. "I said I am a Christian," I replied. "I didn't say I was a prostitute. You see, I have a counseling center on the Lower East Side, and Christ is using me to help people who live down there. I probably know Benny Barnes better than you do. I know he's mean. There was a time several years ago when he tried to kill me. I've gotten a couple of his girls to leave him and go up to the Walter Hoving Home in Garrison. That's a Teen Challenge girls' program. Surely you've heard of Teen Challenge."

They both nodded.

"Well, God used Benny Barnes to save my life a couple of times tonight."

"What?" one of them exclaimed in surprise. "Benny Barnes, saving lives? That just doesn't add up."

"Well, officer, I owe my life to that mean pimp."

They both started scratching their heads, puzzling over what I had just told them. Would they believe it? Then I noticed one staring at my waist again. I was almost positive he knew the gun was hidden there. But I also knew I had no permit for carrying a concealed weapon. If I produced the gun, would I get arrested? Or would the policemen use it as evidence against Benny? But if I didn't produce it and they called in a woman officer to search me, what kind of a Christian testimony would that be? And what would it do to my father? The publicity was something he could well do without. I was really jammed.

"What's your name?" the cop demanded.

"Marji Parker."

"Marji Parker?" he yelled. "Are you the Marji Parker who has the counseling center down on East Eleventh Street?"

I smiled. Thank God he had heard about my work. "That's what I've been trying to tell you," I said.

"Don't you know there's an all-points bulletin out on you?" he asked. "I'll bet there are one hundred cops combing the Lower East Side for you. Your aunt reported you missing. Are you sure you're Marji Parker?"

"Yes. And very much alive, thanks to Benny Barnes."

"Hey, Eric," he said to his partner, who was keeping an eye on Benny in the patrol car, "we've found Marji Parker. Call in and tell headquarters."

The partner grabbed the microphone on his police radio and called in. I heard a voice answer: "Hurray! They've found Marji Parker!"

The two policemen then introduced themselves as Craig Endsley and Eric Hollison. Eric asked me, "Don't you know you're a celebrity? The word's gotten around that you saved one of our men in that shoot-out between the Tattooed Terrors and the Hidden Skulls last evening. You crawled across that filthy street and saved Officer Conklin's life! Did you know that?"

Of course I knew what I had done. But I didn't know that everyone else did.

"The commissioner will probably give you a reward

in the mayor's office," he continued. "You're a celebrity!"

In his excitement, he slapped me on the back—a little too hard. I stumbled forward and drew in my stomach to catch my breath. And as I did, the gun slipped to the pavement!

I gasped. Then the two cops glanced down at the gun. Now I was going to get it! How embarrassing! First I was a celebrity; the next minute I was going to be arrested for carrying a weapon! Any thoughts of fame crumbled at my feet.

"What's that on the ground?" Officer Endsley asked.

I looked first at the gun, then at the patrolman. "That's a gun."

"A gun?" he replied. "I don't see any gun. Eric, do you see a gun?"

Eric came over and looked around, deliberately not looking where the gun was. "Craig, I sure don't see any gun," he said.

Craig went back to the car, and Eric picked up the gun. "We knew that gun was on you," he said. "We watched Benny when we were driving up. Sometimes people think the police are stupid. But as soon as I saw what you two were doing, I knew something was being passed. And I could tell you weren't a willing partner to it. I knew Benny would be up to no good. I sure wish I could have caught him with that gun. Then I would have had something on him."

"I know Benny is bad news," I said, "but way down deep inside he has some real hurts. He's tried to do all sorts of things to me because I've taken some of his girls away. But gradually he's come to respect me. And I'm praying that God will save him from his sins and turn him into a real Apostle Paul."

Eric scratched his head. "You really love that guy, don't you?"

I laughed. "Certainly not as a boyfriend. But I do

have the love of Jesus flowing through my heart, and I just can't stop that flow. And sir, I'd like for you to get saved, too."

As soon as I said that word *saved,* Eric stepped back and began studying the pavement. I suddenly became aware of the presence of God there, as the Holy Spirit witnessed to my spirit that Eric was a backslider.

"Officer Hollison, God just told me something about you," I said. "You used to be a Christian, didn't you? But the going got a little tough, and you dropped out."

He didn't respond. I stood there watching as he shifted from one foot to the other, obviously uncomfortable. Then I noticed tears start to trickle down his cheeks. He pulled out his handkerchief and blew his nose, acting as though a speck of dirt had gotten into his eye.

"Officer Hollison, I may never meet you again. We may go our separate ways. But before we do, why don't you bow your head right here and now and get back to God? We could make this filthy, dirty street God's sanctuary. How about it?"

The other cop came back about then. He was listening closely, and I noticed that he stood there with his eyes closed, almost as if he were praying. Was he away from God, too?

"Officer Endsley, how about you?" I asked.

He opened his eyes and smiled. "I'm a Christian," he told me. "You won't believe this, but last Sunday night at our church we had a special prayer for Eric. We'd been together for some time, but I had asked the Lord to give me a Christian partner to work with. I really like to talk about spiritual things, and I like to work with someone who shares those values and ideals. I can't believe that God is answering my prayer so quickly!"

I put my arm on Officer Hollison's shoulder and said, "God is performing a miracle right here, sir. The events of tonight just didn't happen. They were all part of

God's plan. I despaired of my life tonight, but God spared me—perhaps for only one reason—so that Christ could use me to show His love for you. Right now God wants you more than you will ever know."

Tears brimmed in his eyes again. "Just pray right now," I said. "God is here."

Right there, on that dirty street, Eric Hollison asked Jesus to take full control of his life again and promised he'd serve Him all the days of his life. The beauty of what God had done in forgiving him became so real that he just raised his hands, looked up toward heaven, and started praising the Lord aloud. So did I, and so did Officer Endsley.

As we kept praising the Lord, Benny shouted from the police car, "Hey, you religious nuts, what's going on out there?"

That quickly brought us back to the present. Officer Endsley walked over, opened the back door, and said, "Benny, this is exactly what you need."

I expected Benny to curse him out. But what I heard was, "Yeah, you're right. Maybe someday. But not now."

Officer Hollison walked over, reached into the cruiser, and grabbed Benny's arm. "Benny," he said, "Marji just told me how you saved her life twice tonight—and something else. You may not understand what I'm talking about, but I believe God used you to bring me back to Himself."

Benny brightened. Because he was always one to take advantage of a situation, I anticipated what he was going to say: "Mr. Policeman, didn't you know that I am God's right-hand messenger? I am bringing His message to many people in need. Now I'm going to take the offering."

"Benny," I warned, "I wouldn't make light of this moment. God is going to get you. One of these days you're going to get saved, too."

"Yeah, I know, Marji," he responded meekly. "But not now."

"Benny, someday may be too late," I remonstrated. "You live on the edge of things. God's Spirit is here right now. He's here to set you free!"

Benny laughed. "He's come to set me free? Then how come I have these handcuffs on?"

Eric yanked Benny out of the car. Was he going to push him around again? That surely was no way to win him over.

"Benny, I guess I owe you a favor," Eric said. "So here's one for you."

He pulled out a key and unlocked the handcuffs. "Benny, you're free to go," he said. "But there's a greater freedom you can have in Jesus. The devil's got you handcuffed on the inside, but Jesus wants to set you free—the way He did for me."

"What is this, man?" Benny asked wonderingly. "No cop has ever taken the cuffs off me that way before. Do you mean to tell me I can just walk away?"

The two officers nodded. "Man, this is too much," Benny said. "I mean, just too much."

"Benny," I said, "don't you know that I love you and these two cops love you, too?"

"No way, man; no way!" Benny responded with a laugh. "There's no cop in this city who could ever love me!"

Eric put his arm around him, but Benny wiggled free and jumped back, apparently thinking he would be restrained again. So Officer Hollison playfully wagged his finger at Benny as he said, "Benny, one day I'm going to get you and get you good. I'm not going to get you with a gun. I'm not going to get you with my club. I'm not going to get you with my handcuffs. But I'm going to get you with the Gospel of Jesus Christ. He's going to blast that hard heart of yours to smithereens. And He will

come into your heart and make you something important in His kingdom!"

I expected another of Benny's snide remarks, but he
looked down at the ground, almost as though he was
embarrassed. "Maybe you're right, sir; maybe you're
right," he said softly.

As Benny turned to walk away, Officer Endsley said,
"Hey Benny, we found a gun on the sidewalk. Do you
know whose it is?"

Benny looked at the outstretched hand with the gun,
then at me, then at the cops. "Why don't you keep it?"
he said. "People can get hurt with those things."

With that he walked away, head down, shoulders
slouched. I knew he was under conviction for his sins.
How long would it be, and what would it take, before
Benny Barnes surrendered his heart and life to Jesus?
Oh, how I was praying to see that day!

"Marji, we'd better get you back to your apartment,"
Officer Endsley said as he helped me into the backseat of
the patrol car. "I'm sure the department has been in
touch with your aunt and uncle, but I know they'll be
anxious to see you."

It would be great to get back to the place I called
home. I was absolutely drained. I couldn't believe that
anyone would be able to go through all I had been
through in the past hours!

As we were driving back, I told the officers about my
encounter with the Tattooed Terrors that night and how
every time it seemed I was getting somewhere with
them, the police showed up. I asked them to pray with
me about the situation, because I was convinced the
gangs had decided I was on the side of the police.

Then it hit me. If members of either of those gangs
happened to be on the streets at this hour and saw me
getting out of a police car, that would confirm their
worst suspicions.

But the alternative was to walk through that jungle alone. It was four in the morning, and I'd be easy prey for junkies. What should I do?

About six blocks from my apartment I said, "Men, you're going to have to let me out here. I'll walk the rest of the way."

Eric abruptly turned around. "Marji, you're crazy!" he said. "Even a cop is hardly safe in that jungle. You couldn't go two blocks without getting hit over the head. We've got to deliver you right to your door. It's too dangerous at this time of night for you to be out there alone."

"I appreciate your concern," I said, "and from a human standpoint, I know that what you're saying is true. But God has spared my life twice tonight. I think He'll do it one more time."

"Marji, this is absolutely stupid!" Craig told me.

"I know it seems that way. But I also know that if any of those gang members see me getting out of a police car, I'm in deep trouble. They'll cut me off. I can't take the chance of that happening. I really believe God is trying to do something to stop these foolish gang wars. But if those gang members think I'm in with the police, I'll never be able to reach them. I've got to walk through here alone. There's no other way."

Craig pulled over to the curb. "I guess you're right," he said slowly. "But this really makes me nervous. Let's pray."

If it made him nervous to think about my doing it, you can imagine what it did to me. My heart was beating like crazy in anticipation of that jungle walk!

Then Craig prayed, asking God to protect me so I would arrive safely. He prayed for the two gangs, that somehow I would be able to reach them with the Gospel.

When he finished praying, I felt calmer. I thanked

both of them for their kindness, got out, and started walking down that deserted street.

I didn't hear the police car drive off. The patrolmen must have been sitting there, watching me. *Well,* I thought, *I guess I'll have some protection until I get out of viewing range.*

But any comfort was short-lived. The police car drove on by me and off down the street. When it was out of sight, I looked ahead and noticed a man leaning up against a wall. Was he a mugger? A junkie? Why was he out at this hour of the night?

My heart beat wildly again. Something was wrong. I'd better cross the street to get away from him.

As I did that, he started walking toward me. Quickening my pace, I thought of running. But I knew I would be no match for him, so I stopped and wheeled around. I wasn't going to let him grab me from behind.

"What do you want?" I asked.

He flipped out a badge and said, "I'm a policeman. What are you doing out at this time of night?"

"I'm just walking home, that's all."

"You must be absolutely stupid," he said. "An attractive young lady like you, out at this time of night, must be either crazy or drunk!"

"I'm not drunk, and I don't think I'm crazy," I replied. "I'm a Christian, and I trust God to watch over me while I'm walking to my apartment."

The cop laughed. "Listen, God wouldn't walk these streets at this time of night," he quipped.

At least he had a sense of humor!

"Officer, I really don't have time to explain everything," I said, "but I'm under God's protection. I must go now."

"Well, I think God wants me to walk with you," he said.

"No, please don't do that," I said. "That might ruin

everything. I insist on walking alone."

"Lady, let me smell your breath. You have to be drunk."

"No sir, I am not drunk. I know what I'm doing. I don't really like to do it, but I must walk home alone."

He shrugged. "Okay lady, have it your way. I'm supposed to be here to protect people. But if you don't want protection, there's really nothing I can do. Go your way."

"Thank you, sir. I know you don't understand this, but God does. My life is in His hands."

"You certainly must have a big God."

I smiled. What a beautiful reminder for building my faith—and it came from someone who really didn't understand what he had said!

Reassured of God's protection, I started on my way. About fifty paces away, I turned and waved. He was still standing there in the middle of the street, watching me. I'm sure he thought I had to be the most stupid person alive.

I walked two more blocks and turned to see whether he was still following. He wasn't. But when I looked ahead, I saw someone else—a younger-looking man, maybe a teenager.

He just stood there as I walked by. But a sixth sense I had developed from living in this area told me I was being followed. I glanced back. Sure enough, he was following me. But when he saw me look, he tried to melt into the darkness and act as though he wasn't even aware I was around.

I quickened my pace. Was he a junkie? A mugger? Was I being foolish for walking through here alone? Why hadn't I thought of having the police call a cab to take me home? Maybe I was presuming on God's protection.

Well, it was too late to worry about those things now! My immediate problem was that kid who was following me. Where were those cops when I needed them?

I began to run, but I could hear his footsteps getting closer and closer on this strangely quiet street.

I glanced over my shoulder and saw his open switchblade glisten under a streetlight!

8

When I saw his switchblade flashing under the street-light, I whirled around to face the attacker. If he was going to kill me, it wasn't going to be by stabbing me in the back! I would try to protect myself as well as I could; but if I lost, that was the Lord's problem, not mine.

Planting my feet squarely, I looked at him and demanded, "What do you want?"

He bared his teeth and hissed at me, just like a rat. I immediately knew he must be a member of the Tattooed Terrors. But how had he gotten out of jail so soon? Hadn't they even been kept overnight?

"It's all over for you, Marji Parker," he snarled. "You'd better get down on your knees and say a little prayer, after what you did to my friends."

"What do you mean by that?" I asked. "What did I do wrong?"

"Get down on your knees!" he commanded again. "I'm not kidding. You'd better say your final prayer!"

I just stood there, so he screamed it out: "I said get down on your knees, and I mean it!"

What better way to die? I dropped to my knees.

"Start praying, preacher lady; start praying!"

He didn't need to tell me to pray. I was already doing that. And I was ready to die, if that was what God wanted. I only hoped it would be quick.

He grabbed my hair and twisted it, pulling my face

up. Then he jammed his switchblade under my chin, spitting out the words, "I'm going to kill you, you dirty double-crosser!"

With a far greater calmness than I felt, I looked at him and said, "Kill me, then."

He jabbed the switchblade until the point pierced my skin. Oh, how it stung! I tried to jerk away, but he held me fast.

"I'm going to start by cutting your tongue out," he said. "But you have such a long, fat tongue that I'm going to have to go the long way to be sure I get it all out. I'm going to have to start down here in your throat!"

I gritted my teeth and thought what a horrible way this was to die. But if it would bring glory and honor to God, then I was ready.

I looked into the boy's eyes, and I will never forget what I saw there as long as I live. It was just as if I were looking into the face of the devil! Such hatred; such loathing; such wickedness! I realized that I wasn't simply confronting a teenage gang member. This was, as the Bible says, a spiritual warfare! I was in hand-to-hand combat with Satan!

"Before you kill me, why don't you tell me why you're doing it?" I said.

"You know why," he snarled. "You're a cop lover. That's what you are—a cop lover! You're the one who framed us. Because of you, you double-crosser, all the rest of my gang members are in jail right now."

"Now wait a minute!" I protested. "I didn't call any cops."

"Tell me another lie!" he shouted. "You're the one who called those cops. You set up that whole thing. You think you're so smart—that you know what's better for us than we do ourselves. You'll never convince me you didn't call those cops. And now you're going to die for it!"

With that, he pulled the knife away from my throat, holding it back as though he was about to stab me with it.

"Jesus loves you, son," I blurted out.

His other hand hit hard across my face, almost knocking me to the pavement. While I was trying to regain my balance, he grabbed my hair again and jerked me to my feet.

"I'm not going to kill you right this minute," he announced grandly. "I'm going to give you a chance. Here's my deal. You bail out all my gang members, and I'll believe you didn't set this thing up. You don't bail them out, and I'm going to get you."

"Do you realize what you're asking?" I said. "There must have been at least seventy-five of those boys arrested. It would take thousands of dollars to get them out. I don't have that kind of money."

"Don't talk to me about money," he sneered. "We all read in the papers about the kind of money your old man was willing to pay to ransom you from those kidnappers. If your old man has got that kind of money, he can bail out all the Tattooed Terrors. He'd better do it, if he wants to see you alive again!"

I guess the whole Lower East Side knew about my kidnapping, and that I came from an extremely wealthy family. I thank God for delivering me in that incident. But it did have an effect upon my ministry because now everybody thought of me as a rich man's kid. And that didn't help down here, among this abject poverty.

"What makes you so sure I can get the money from my dad?"

"Listen, preacher lady, you just take this message to him. Either he'll cough up that bail money, or he'll go to your funeral. I think he'll understand that. I've signed an oath in my own blood that I will die for the freedom of my brothers. I heard you hadn't made it home yet, so I decided to wait. I'm going to kill you,

Marji Parker. I'm going to kill you if you don't get that bail money!"

Racing through my mind were thoughts about what to do. My dad hadn't been excited about my coming to the Lower East Side, and I had decided long ago that I shouldn't be here without his permission. If he knew some gang members were threatening my life, would he make me pull out of here and leave my counseling center? I just couldn't take that chance.

The boy grabbed my hair and jerked my chin back again. Once more I felt his switchblade prick my skin. "Are you going to do what I say?" he asked insistently.

I didn't want to go to Dad, but I didn't want to lie to this boy, either. "I'll do my best," I finally said. "I'll do what I can."

That enraged him. He jabbed the knife against my chin and then pulled it back to show me my blood on its tip. "This whole blade will be covered with your blood if you don't get that bail money!" He wiped the blade against his jeans and, folding it, stuck it back in his pocket. I guess he figured he'd made his point.

"I said I would try, and I will," I told him.

"You do better than that!" he threatened.

"Hey, how come you're not in jail?" I asked.

He hissed, "Those cops are stupid. I could have killed six of them easily when they broke into our headquarters."

"Maybe God stopped you from doing that."

"Nobody stopped me. I was afraid some of my brothers might get hurt. You see, I was on the floor above you. Three of us were up there—backup protection, you know? Even though our four lookouts got busted, the cops didn't know about the three of us just above them. We were all set to pull our triggers, but there were too many cops this time; too many of our brothers would have been killed, too. In fact, I had my gun aimed at you, and another brother had his aimed at Benny

Barnes. All Ratface had to do was wrinkle his nose, and you wouldn't be here now."

I wondered why Ratface hadn't given that order. He certainly had acted as though he wanted to kill me!

"Now you'd better get that bail money!" he threatened again.

"Okay, I'll do my best," I answered, at the same time wondering what the police would say if I appeared to bail out the Tattooed Terrors—especially now that I was being celebrated as the heroine of the New York City Police Department!

He screamed at me again, "You're going to do more than your best, or it's all over for you!"

I'd had just about as much of this as I was going to take from him. "Young man," I said, wagging my finger at his face, "I don't know who you are, but I think it's time we got a few things straight. First, I'm not afraid to die. If you want to, take that switchblade out of your pocket and plunge it right through my heart. As far as I'm concerned, it's up to God whether I live or die. I'm prepared for that eventuality. I know I'll die someday. But my greatest fear isn't for me; it's for you. If you kill me, they'll probably catch you, and you'll do time as a murderer. But even worse than that, you are already under a death sentence. You'll die and go to hell if you don't get right with God!"

He hissed, "I'm not afraid to die. I'm a Tattooed Terror!"

Just then, I heard footsteps and looked down the street. Approaching us was that plainclothes cop. He quickly walked up and asked, "What seems to be the problem here?"

Now I had this Tattooed Terror. One word from me, and he would join his fellow gang members in jail. All I had to do was suggest to that cop that he frisk him. He'd find the switchblade, and the kid would be arrested on a concealed-weapons charge. Or I could file a complaint of attempted murder. All I had to do was point to the wound in my chin.

Since nobody answered, the policeman turned his attention to me and asked, "Ma'am, are you all right?"

The gang member started backing away. Then the cop whipped out his gun and yelled, "Hold it!"

The boy threw his hands high in the air as the cop asked me again, "Any problem?"

"No, officer," I replied, "We were just having a little religious discussion about life and death."

The gang member hissed and started backing up again.

"I said hold it!" the officer yelled.

The kid stopped, his hands still held high.

"I'm going to ask one more time, ma'am. Is there some kind of a problem here?"

Oh, I was tempted to blurt out the whole situation. It riled my righteous indignation to think that punks like this kid were getting away with murder on the city streets. But I knew that even if I got this fellow arrested, he still had two friends loose on the streets. Eventually one of them would find a way to get me. And I never would be able to reach this gang if I were responsible for one of their members' being in jail. They blamed me for that now, even though I had had nothing to do with it. I had to keep on trusting God to change these people; that would do what no jail term would ever be able to accomplish!

"No, sir," I replied, "just a friendly little encounter."

The gang member kept edging away. Finally the cop said, "Okay, kid, scram! Get out of here before I run you in!"

The kid spun around and ran like the wind down the street. Then the cop turned back toward me and asked, "Do you know who that was?"

"Yes," I answered. "He's a member of the Tattooed Terrors."

"You'd better believe it," he said, apparently surprised that I knew it. "But if you knew he was a gang member, why did you tell me it was a friendly encounter. You're not a member of that gang, too, are you?"

I laughed nervously. "I wish I could infiltrate them," I responded. "I'd like to get them all straightened out, but I don't think they'd let me join."

"Ma'am, I just can't figure you out. All you would have to have done was say the word, and I would have run that punk in. I know he's up to no good. You're lucky he didn't kill you."

"Some people might call it luck," I responded, "but I call it God's protection. I guess it just wasn't my time to die. But when it is, I know I'll meet Jesus."

"Oh, wow! I've got another religious fanatic on my hands!"

"I guess you might call me that," I said. "But the longer I'm up tonight, the more positive I am that God has a specific mission for me to fulfill among these gangs. It's not over yet."

"Lady, you just aren't adding up."

"No, I suppose I'm not," I mused. "I guess you're new down here. I run a counseling center on East Eleventh. Come by sometime, and I'll explain to you what I mean. Okay? Now I really must be getting home."

"Wait a minute!" he exploded. "I'm not about to have to investigate any murder tonight. I'm about ready to go off duty. If something happens to you, that mean's I'll have a lot of paperwork to take care of. So I'm going to walk you to your apartment.".

I didn't protest. If any of the Tattooed Terrors were around, they would have seen me with the cop by this time. And they would have known that I hadn't called him. So I said, "I guess that'll be okay, if it will relieve your fears."

"Relieve my fears?" he asked in surprise. "Aren't you scared out here all by yourself?"

"I've got plenty of company."

"What? I've tailed you. The only other person I saw on these streets was that gang member. So what do you mean, you've got plenty of company?"

"Well, as I told you, I'm a Christian. And I really believe God has His guardian angels watching over me. They're with me right now."

The cop looked up and down the street, then up into the air. "I don't see any angels anywhere."

"Of course not," I said, laughing. "These are the unseen angels of God whom the Bible says watch over us."

"Lady, I'm sure you're sincere," he said, "but if you don't stop talking that way, I'm going to have to run you in. Now let me get you home."

"Okay. Two blocks and I'm there."

The policeman didn't say anything as we walked those two blocks. Every once in a while I would catch him looking at me, apparently trying to figure me out. I wondered if he would ever take up my offer to stop at the counseling center.

"Well, here we are," I announced. "Thanks for walking me home. And may the angels of God go with you."

He laughed. "I could sure use an angel or two in my job," he replied. "My backup buddy, who walks a block away, sometimes falls asleep. So if you get an angel for me, get me one who stays awake!"

I giggled at his attempt at humor, but I hoped he realized I was indeed serious. I knew the angels of God were with me. They had to have been. And they certainly had had to work overtime that night!

When I unlocked the apartment door, I saw the light on in the kitchen. Amilda called, "Is that you, Marji?" and then my aunt and uncle came running, gathering me into their arms and hugging and kissing me and exclaiming over and over, "Thank God you're safe! Thank God you're safe!"

"Uncle Alex, you had doubt about me?" I teased.

He smiled back. We were always chiding one another about a lack of faith, so I had him on this one.

"You know how it is," he said. "I thought maybe heaven needed another saint and decided on you. But I guess it didn't need another one tonight and gave you a rain check!"

We all laughed. Then all three of us started talking at once. Aunt Amilda gently took me by the arm and led me to the kitchen table. "The police called and told us you were safe," she said as she poured me some coffee. "And you'll never believe how many other calls we've had. They've been coming in all night. It's all about your rescuing that policeman. Would you believe a photographer for the *Daily News* was at the shoot-out? He monitored the police radio and got there before it ever started. Well, he got a picture of you and Officer Conklin, who was injured. Your picture's going to be in the paper tomorrow. You're a celebrity!"

They wanted to know everything that had happened, so I started telling them about it from the moment Benny and I had walked into the headquarters of the Tattooed Terrors to our being rescued there by the cops to our being abducted by Cobra and rescued by some more policemen. They rejoiced as I told them how Officer Hollison got saved on the street. But I wondered if I ought to tell them about my most recent encounter with the member of the Tattooed Terrors.

I guess as I thought of that encounter, it must have showed on my face, because Aunt Amilda asked, "Marji, is something bothering you? You look as white as a sheet."

I looked straight at her and said, "Yes, Aunt Amilda. My life has been threatened again."

"What now?" Alex demanded.

"It's still the Tattooed Terrors."

"I thought they were all in jail," Amilda said.

"Not quite. All but three. I encountered one of them

out on the street about two blocks from here. He claims he'll kill me if I don't go to Dad and get bail money to get all those gang members out of jail."

"What?" Alex responded. "That's absolutely preposterous!"

"I know it seems that way," I said, "but that's what he wants. And I really believe he will kill me if I don't do it."

Aunt Amilda stared at the floor. Then she said, almost in tears, "Maybe God will let you be killed so that others will come down here and help out in this ministry. It may take that, Marji."

"Oh, Aunt Amilda, don't talk that way," I chided. "If God got me out of all these other messes, He'll get me out of this one, too. I just know He will."

"Now wait a minute, Marji," she said. "It seems to me that when we were talking about this subject just after I got saved, you told me about five missionaries who were ambushed and brutally murdered by Indians in South America. A lot of people thought that was a terrible tragedy, a waste of young lives. But as a result of their deaths, thousands of young people surrendered their lives to be missionaries. God may want to do something like that with you to let the people of America know of the hundreds of thousands of people in our cities who are lost and going to hell."

I knew that was a distinct possibility. It did seem as though little was said in the churches about the mission field of the ghettos. I tried, but it was awfully hard to challenge people to come down there and reach out to those who were so desperately in need. But neither was I too excited about the prospect of being a martyr!

"Aunt Amilda, do you have the mind of God?" I asked.

She smiled. "Marji, I heard someone once say—I forget who it was—that the highest calling for any Christian is not to be an evangelist or a missionary or a great preacher; the highest calling is to be a martyr."

I wasn't sure I agreed. I'd heard someone else say it was sometimes harder to live for God than it was to die for Him!

But I also knew Aunt Amilda was right on one score: If God wanted to call me to be a martyr, I had to be willing. "If God wants to use my death to get people to rise to the challenge of the inner city, I want to be willing to die for Him," I said.

Uncle Alex chimed in, "I'd be honored, too, if God wanted me to die as a martyr."

Aunt Amilda drew us both close and began to pray: "Lord Jesus, please forgive us for our weak faith. We know that gang members filled with hate form a pact unto death. We have You, the Giver of life and peace. We solemnly swear to You that if You should call us to be martyrs, we humbly accept that honor. Take away fear; put in faith. And help us to work like we've never worked for You before. We know You will come back. But when You do, may each of us be found working to the best of our abilities to reach all these people who are hurting for You. In Your name. Amen."

Suddenly I felt better about the whole situation. "You know," I said, "it's absolutely amazing what happens to your spirit when you accept the will of God for your life. Often I'm afraid to die, but not now. The question has been settled in my heart. I'm now ready to be that 'living sacrifice.' "

Uncle Alex slapped me on the back and exclaimed, "Wouldn't it be wonderful if we all died together? Then, in the twinkling of an eye, we'd all be in heaven! Think of it!"

Aunt Amilda smiled. "The way things have been going around this neighborhood," she said, "that may not be too long!"

I headed down the hall to my bedroom—finally to get

some rest. It seemed a little stuffy in the room, so I decided to open the window. When I did, I heard a blood-curdling scream. It seemed to be coming from the burned-out tenement across the street.

I tore out of that bedroom, back to the kitchen, calling, "Did you hear that scream?"

"I sure did!" Alex replied. "Where was it coming from?"

"I'm not sure, but it seemed to be coming from right across the street. No one would be in that building, would they?"

"Let's take a look," Uncle Alex suggested.

The three of us walked to my bedroom and over to the window, straining to see through the predawn darkness. Then we heard that hideous scream again.

Alex pushed us back, ordering, "Everybody down!" We all quickly obeyed.

"There's somebody across the street with a rifle pointed right this way," he said.

"Who? Who?" I asked.

"I'm pretty sure it's a member of the Tattooed Terrors."

"But why? Why?"

"I'm sure it's a scare tactic. He's screaming as though he were a rat. He'll probably stay there until the other gang members are bailed out of jail. Or else he's planning to shoot you, Marji."

I started trembling all over. A few minutes ago I had said I was willing to be a martyr. But when that Tattooed Terror seemed willing to make me one, I wasn't all that willing!

Uncle Alex jumped up to pull down the shade, but he pulled too hard, and it clattered to the floor. I thought I'd been shot!

I noticed Aunt Amilda trembling, too; I wasn't the only one who was afraid.

Uncle Alex noticed our nervousness and chided, "Fine Christians you are! I thought we were all willing to die together."

"I'm willing, but I'm not anxious!" I responded. "But if you're so full of faith, why don't you stand in the window and hang that shade back up? Then raise your fist defiantly at the man across the street. Then we'll see how much faith you have!"

Looking his most serious, Uncle Alex said, "Marji, this is no game. God doesn't want us to act foolishly to prove we have faith. That's presumption!"

I nodded. I knew he was right.

"Now I'll tell you what's likely to happen in this situation," he went on. "You've already been told about the death threat. He won't try anything right now. But in a day or two, if you haven't gotten those gang members out of jail, he'll try to kill you. So I think we really ought to try to figure out some plan of action that we think God wants us to take. This is serious."

I apologized for being flippant. Then we all crawled out of the bedroom and out of sight of the sniper across the street. I suggested we all try to get some sleep before we worked on a plan of action.

As I settled on the living-room sofa to try to sleep, that bloodcurdling scream once again ripped through the air. I wondered how long it would be before the gang member would take his first shot at me. Did I have just one more day to live?

9

Suddenly I became aware that Uncle Alex was bending over me. "Marji, Marji," he was saying, shaking me gently. "There's a call for you. It's your father."

I was so groggy that my first response was, "What time is it?"

"It's ten o'clock. You've been sleeping about four hours."

I headed toward the phone, being careful to put a smile in my voice, even though I was still dog tired.

Dad's voice came into my ear. "Marji, what in the world have you been up to? Have you seen the papers?"

"No, I was up rather late last night," I said, in what had to be one of the world's great understatements.

"Well, get yourself a copy of the *Daily News*. Go to the centerfold. You won't believe what's there!"

I had a pretty good idea.

"Marji, was this a publicity stunt? Are you trying to raise finances for your center? Why didn't you just come to me?"

Dad had always been willing to help with the finances. But I didn't like to depend on him. And I had no idea how he would respond to the idea of bail for those gang members.

"Marji, I also received a call from Mr. McNeil, the police commissioner. He invited your mother and me to be his special guests at an award ceremony at three today down at City Hall."

"An award ceremony? What kind of an award ceremony?"

"Haven't you heard? They plan to give you the highest medal of honor here in New York City because you saved that policeman's life!"

"They want to give *me* an award?" I asked in surprise. "I don't need anything like that. I just did what seemed to be the right thing."

"Well, I'm proud of your courage, of course," Dad went on. "But those gang wars down there in the Lower East Side really worry me—especially right there in front of your counseling center. I think maybe you should get out of there for a while and come home and rest. We can talk about it when we see you this afternoon."

"Now, Daddy," I replied. "You don't need to worry about me. God has His hand over me, protecting me. And in that situation I just crawled out on the pavement to help a policeman who had been hurt. It was no big deal."

"That's what you think!" he responded. "Commissioner McNeil told me all about that horrible shoot-out between the Tattooed Terrors and the Hidden Skulls. He said it was one of the worst battles ever in the city! The report he got from his officers said that you crawled out there with bullets whizzing all around you and rescued that man. I think they even plan to make you an honorary member of the police department!"

He couldn't hide the note of pride in his voice.

Then the implication of what he was telling me hit me. If the gang members heard I had been made an honorary policeman, I'd never be able to reach them with the Gospel!

"Dad," I said, "I don't think I'd better go to that award ceremony. I just don't want that kind of recognition. It might hurt my work down here."

"Nonsense, Marji," he responded. "I've been thinking

about that, and it might be the best possible thing for your work. You see, when you receive that award, it will be publicized. I know the *New York Times* plans to have a reporter there. So does *People* magazine. The TV people will be there with their cameras. It might even make the networks. Now when people hear about your work, I think you'll have volunteers from all over coming down to work with those poor people down there. And then you will be able to come back and work for me. I've still got that top-management slot open for you. You could work for me and still go down there once in a while to see how—"

"Dad," I interrupted, "we've been through that plan before. I'm not looking for an easy way of life. I belong down here with these people. This is where God wants me."

"You sound just like your mother," he complained. "It seems to me that's all she talks about lately—helping people come to Jesus. We went to see a Broadway play, and she was passing out those religious tracts to the junkies. Oh, it was so embarrassing!"

Good old Mom. Ever since she'd gotten saved, her burden for sinners kept getting bigger and bigger and bigger. Sometimes I wished she would come down and work with me. But even more, I wished that Daddy would give his heart to Jesus.

"Well, I really don't know what to do," I said. "Do you think I should accept the award? Do you think the publicity will help my work?"

"Honey, I don't think you've got any choice," he told me. "You've got to accept it. Our police department is the finest. If they want to honor you in this way, I think you have a responsibility to accept it. You wouldn't want to offend them."

"Okay, Dad, I'll be at the award ceremony. But I'm not even considering the position in your company."

"Do you want me to arrange a ticker-tape parade

down Fifth Avenue?" he teased.

"Oh, Daddy, don't even talk that way! In fact, if I had my choice, I wouldn't even go down to City Hall. Sometimes an award means obligations that can stifle the work of God. The most important thing to me right now is the people who live here on the Lower East Side."

Really, the most important immediate thing was those gang members' bail. If they didn't get out, this was probably the end of my ministry. Something stopped me from asking Dad for the money, yet I still had no idea where I could get it.

After I hung up the phone, Uncle Alex explained that the mayor's office had called earlier but he hadn't awakened me to tell me. A limousine was being sent for us to get us to the 3:00 P.M. award ceremony.

That afternoon, as I walked into City Hall, I was met by two reporters. They wanted to know what motivated me to rescue the policeman. I tried to explain that it was just love and human concern. Then one reporter asked me if it had been a gang member out there injured, would I have done the same thing? When I said, "Yes, certainly!" a couple of people raised their eyebrows. Did they think all gang members ought to be dead?

The award ceremony was rather exciting, but I knew the built-in dangers of taking the credit. So with TV cameras whirring, I had a perfect chance to share my faith in Christ and how God had helped me save an officer's life.

After the ceremony, the mayor invited me into his private office. After being sure I was comfortably situated in a leather chair, he said, "Miss Parker, I wanted to have this little one-to-one chat before you leave. Your father is quite concerned about what happened down there. You probably know he is a major contributor to my election campaign, and I hold him in high esteem, so we know each other quite well. I know he is proud of you—he as much as told me that—but he is also afraid that one of these days you're going to be killed by a nut who has flipped out or by those gang members. I don't need to tell you that the problems these gangs are creating are becoming more and more difficult to solve. The police are working night and day, trying to keep some of those crazy kids alive. They've become a real menace to their neighborhoods."

"Well, Mr. Mayor, I live down there among all those problems. I know my father fears for my safety. I suppose he told you about the kidnapping."

"He didn't have to tell me about that. That was in all the papers. I guess he has to pay a big penalty, the way I do. I can't go out in public without police protection. I guess he needs that kind of protection because of his business. Do you have protection, too?"

"No, I haven't. That's a deal Dad and I made before I went to the Lower East Side: no police protection; no private detectives. I knew I couldn't gain the confidence of the people, otherwise."

"Say, you really take your chances then, don't you?"

"Oh, I have guards. You see, the Lord sends His angels to guard me."

"Angels? You mean you really believe God sends angels?"

"Yes, sir. That's what the Bible says, and I believe the Bible."

"Do you think I could hire a few of them?" the mayor asked with a chuckle. "That is, providing they don't organize and strike for higher pay."

I joined his laughter. Then he got serious. "Miss Parker, you must have a lot of needs. Oh, I don't mean for personal things. I'm sure your father takes care of those things. What I mean is this: Is there anything we can do for you down on the Lower East Side?"

What an opening! What could the city of New York do for me?

"Maybe we could go in there and open up a job-training program near your center," he said. "Maybe that would help get some of the unemployed youth off the streets."

"Well, that's important," I said. "Some of the fellows we've been able to help we've sent to the Teen Challenge training center. That's what they call their farm for boys in Rehrersburg, Pennsylvania. Not only do they receive spiritual help there but they also are trained in various vocations. The boys learn about mechanics, body-shop work, printing—even farming."

"Well, I don't think it would be feasible to start a farm on the Lower East Side. But it may not be a bad idea. We could knock down some of those burned-out tenements and plant a pasture. But do you think anyone would know how to milk a cow?"

We both laughed again. He certainly was easy to talk to.

"Maybe we could send in a teacher and set up a secretarial course for the girls you are helping."

The mayor's ideas were good, but they didn't seem to be the real answer to the problems of the Lower East Side. I breathed a quick prayer for wisdom in knowing what to ask.

And the answer hit me like a bolt out of heaven. Something—I believe it was God—told me to ask him to release those members of the Tattooed Terrors! But I staggered a little just at the idea of asking such a thing.

"What's the matter?" the mayor asked me. "Are you feeling faint?"

"Oh, no," I responded. "I just had an idea. I don't know whether it's something you can do, but I guess it won't hurt to ask."

"Let me guess," the mayor said. "You want a bigger building to take in all the people who will be coming to you now that you've become famous."

Blushing slightly, I said, "No, that's not it. But what I

would like to ask is that you arrange for the release of the members of the Tattooed Terrors who are being held in jail."

"What?" the mayor responded in surprise. "You want me to have those hoodlums released?"

"Maybe they're really not hoodlums, sir. Maybe they just haven't had a chance. Maybe nobody has ever shown any confidence in them. Sir, I'd really like to see them released. Is that possible?"

He scratched his chin and then laughed. "Can't you just see the headlines if I do that? 'Mayor releases gang members to roam streets once more.' They might even accuse me of joining a gang! No, Miss Parker, I don't think I could do something like that."

I was sure God had been directing me, so I wasn't about to give up easily.

"Mr. Mayor, you know that jail isn't going to do those kids any good. You know what they learn from the other prisoners: bad things. And when they are released, they go right back on the streets and do what they did before—maybe even worse things."

He rubbed his chin again. "You're a very perceptive person, Miss Parker," he replied. "I can see a lot of your father's characteristics in you. And you're right in what you're saying." He paused. "But why is it so important to you that I release those particular gang members?"

That was a question I was hoping he wouldn't ask! If I told him, I just knew he'd go right to my father, and that would end my ministry on the Lower East Side. I just couldn't take a chance on that happening.

"Oh, I just love people, Mr. Mayor, and I want to help them."

"Miss Parker, I don't work around a lot of people without learning a few things about human nature. And something tells me there is a lot more to this situation than what you've just said. Now tell me the real reason."

I just couldn't bring myself to do that, and now I was really trapped. I offered another quick prayer. Thank God for prayer!

"Are you in love with one of those gang members?" the mayor teased.

"Well, I must admit a couple of them are quite handsome," I replied, smiling. "But that's not my reason."

"Miss Parker, come over and sit down on this sofa, please."

I could hear the reporters still stirring around out in the hall, waiting to talk to us. And I was positive the first thing they'd want to know was what the mayor and I talked about. I sure didn't want them to get hold of that death threat on me!

The mayor sat on one end of the sofa; I sat on the other. He leaned toward me and said, "Miss Parker, I don't know whether or not I can talk to you the way your own father does. I don't really know what kind of a relationship you have with your father. But I'm a father; I have three beautiful daughters myself, who are just a little younger than you. As I've come to know about the things you've accomplished in the Lower East Side, I can't help but have great respect for you. I pass through those areas often. I see the hurting people. I see the poverty. I see the run-down buildings, some of them in ruins. I see the people hanging around the streets because they can't get work. I see the vacant hopelessness in their faces. And I read the statistics: murders, rapes, stealings, drugs. Miss Parker, that area where you work is hell on earth. I really respect anyone who can do anything down there. The award we've given you for saving the life of one of our officers is really insignificant compared with the work you're doing."

I was getting embarrassed that he was so complimentary.

"I know there's got to be something behind your

wanting those gang members released," he went on. "Could I make one request?"

"Certainly, Mr. Mayor. I'll try to give you whatever you want of me, God helping me."

"Then, Miss Parker, trust me, will you please? Just trust me."

"What do you mean by that?"

He smiled. "Why don't you tell me why you want those gang members released, and then let me help you solve the problem? Not only am I the mayor and have the powers of this city at my disposal but I'm also very human. I've given a lot of thought to those gang members today. Suppose one of them were my son. I know a little about the terrible conditions those people live in. Those kids don't really have a chance. Many of them don't know who their parents are. I've got misdirected people who cry out that we should kill them. But we can't go in there and do that. They're frustrated and bitter and mad at the world. They need help. And I really want to help them the way you want to help them." He leaned toward me, his voice betraying his eagerness: "I really do, Miss Parker."

His voice cracked with emotion, and he dabbed a tear from his eye.

"Mr. Mayor, you really love the people of this city, don't you?"

"I really do, Miss Parker—and especially those who live on the Lower East Side."

I saw another tear roll down his cheek. He certainly seemed to be a compassionate man. The Spirit of God convicted me right then of not praying for him regularly as I knew a Christian should do.

"Miss Parker, I grew up on the Lower East Side," he said. "My parents were immigrants from Italy. You can imagine what we had to go through, living down there. But we made it. My dad finally got a good-paying job, and we had to move away from the Lower East Side because it was falling apart. But my heart is still there with those suffering people. I've been through there many times, and it's a pain I almost cannot bear."

I thanked God for the insight I was gaining into the mayor's personality. I'm afraid I hadn't paid much attention to politics. I thought all politicians were out to line their own pockets and use power for their own purposes. But this one certainly wasn't that way, and there must be many others around the country just like him.

But suppose I told him why I wanted the gang members released. Would he report that to my dad? I had to do something, since he was so insistent about the real reason.

"Mr. Mayor, you've asked me to trust you. Now may I ask you a favor?"

"Well, Miss Parker, that's what we've been trying to get at in these last few minutes. Of course you can. And I'll try to do it, as you say, God helping me."

"Well, I've asked you to get the gang members out. But there's another request that is important to me. If you're able to do that, please don't tell my father. In fact, don't let anybody know. Even if the gang members themselves knew I was behind it, they're so suspicious that they'd think I did it to set them up to get killed."

"I can understand all that, Miss Parker. But you still haven't told me why you want them released."

"Okay, I'll lay it all out before you. The Tattooed Terrors have a death threat out on me. They've told me that if I don't get those gang members out on bail, they'll kill me. In fact, right across from my apartment, a sniper is staked out on the roof of a burned-out tenement. He's part of the Tattooed Terrors and has told me he'll kill me if I don't come through."

"So that's it," the mayor said, starting toward his telephone. "Well, I'll take care of that right now. I'll have our men go up there and get that kid. He's breaking the law. We'll get him right away."

I jumped up and exclaimed, "No! No! That is exactly what I *don't* want to happen! If we use violence against violence, a bunch of people are going to get killed. All I want you to do, if it's within your power, is to release those gang members. Let me take it from there."

"But Miss Parker, releasing them won't solve anything. They'll be right back on the streets. I don't know whether you understand this or not, but a lot of them really have no homes to go to. They have to eat, so they steal. Their self-image has been destroyed, so they develop an image of power and ruthlessness. If I release them, they'll go right back on the streets, fighting and killing." He shook his head.

"Something else," he added. "You'll never make a deal with them. They'll make all sorts of death threats to get what they want. And when they get out, they'll still try to kill you, Miss Parker. I know that for sure."

"Mr. Mayor, you've missed my point. Everything you've said is probably true. But I'm asking for a chance for those kids—a chance for me to win them to Jesus Christ. I still believe God has helped me and spared my life several times in the last few days because He wants me to help stop the war between those gangs. But I can't really help them when they're in jail."

"It seems like a foolish idea to me," he said.

"I know it seems foolish. But I had a good talk with the Lord about it. I'm not anxious to die, but I told Him I was willing to give my life if it would mean these people could be helped in some way. So if they kill me, they kill me. But I've got to take the chance with them on the street. That's where I have to meet them."

"But Miss Parker, suppose something goes wrong?" he protested. "Suppose I get them released, and they kill you? What then? If your dad ever found out what I had done, my career would be ended. The newspaper and TV reporters would have a field day writing about my releasing those gang members and then you, our newest heroine, being killed as a result of my decision. And they'd call it a stupid decision. I can't go along with this; I really can't. I must call your father and discuss it with him."

He turned toward the door. Now I was stuck. I'd really blown it. He had asked me to trust him. I did—and now this!

"Mr. Mayor, before you go out there, would it be possible for us to have a word of prayer together? I really need to consult God about this. I think my career is about over."

"What do you mean by that?" he asked in surprise.

"When my dad finds out my life has been threatened, he'll force me to leave the Lower East Side. I'll be gone, but the gang wars will continue; the dope pushers will be after every innocent kid down there; the pimps will have the run of the streets. I'll be living in isolated, sterile security out on our Long Island estate. But my career will be over."

"Now wait a minute! Aren't you being overly dramatic?"

"I don't think so. You know my dad and how strong willed he is. He's always been a strict disciplinarian and doesn't want anything to happen to his darling little daughter. I know what he'll do."

"You've really got me over a barrel, haven't you?" the mayor asked.

"No, I don't. I just want to talk to God and see what He says about this. Maybe it's what He wants."

He bowed his head, and I prayed: "Heavenly Father, I thank You first of all for the award. It wasn't me; it was really You who crawled out with me to save that police officer. And now I return the praise and glory to You. I owe it all to You. I thank You for Your friend and mine, the mayor. You said in Your Word that the authorities in government are the messengers of God. Thank You for this messenger You've given to govern our city. I thank You that he has a love and concern for the people of our city. Give him wisdom; direct him. And Lord, I also pray for those gang members who are behind bars today. As they are reaching out, searching for answers to life, help me to bring them that answer in Jesus' name.

"And now, Father, I pray concerning whether or not I am to continue my work on the Lower East Side. I believe the devil is trying to stop it, and I believe You want it to continue. I ask for divine wisdom in this decision. Would You please speak to the mayor's heart and show him what he should do? And Lord, I submit myself to Your will. If it is Your will for me to leave the Lower East Side, then I will. But if it is Your will for me to stay, then I trust that Your angels will continue to be around me.

"Again, Lord, I ask for wisdom in solving the problem of getting those gang members out of jail and telling my father what has happened. Amen."

When I looked up, the mayor had tears rolling down his cheeks. "Miss Parker," he said, "I've never heard a more beautiful prayer."

"Mr. Mayor, you can have God's help in your life. He's got a lot of wisdom for you if you'll just trust Him."

He smiled. "Maybe someday. But I know one thing for sure. If I ever need someone to pray for me, I know whom I'll call!"

Then he added, "Okay, we'll walk out there together. I'll say that you prayed for me, that you asked God's blessings upon New York City, and New York City shall remain the greatest city in the world! And that's all I'm saying."

I smiled. I just knew that God had answered.

"I'll do my best to get those gang members out of jail," he went on. "Even mayors can't work miracles, but I can talk to the judge; maybe they can be released on their own recognizance. They'll still have to come back for a court appearance, but I think we can work out something within the law."

I wrapped my arms around him and squeezed him tightly. "Dad," I said, "you're the greatest!"

He patted my shoulders and said, "Well, I guess my wife and I just gained another daughter. That's four!"

I grabbed him again and kissed him on the cheek. Then I laughed and warned, "Whatever you do, Dad, don't tell them I kissed you, or those reporters will really have something to write about!"

As he opened the door, there stood all those reporters with note pads, pencils, bright lights, and whirring TV cameras.

The mayor stepped forward. I held my breath. Would he be able to stay with what we had agreed upon? Or would some sharp reporter trick him into telling about that death threat? If that happened, I might as well start packing to leave the Lower East Side right now!

10

I squinted against the blinding TV lights, but the mayor, obviously accustomed to them, stepped beside me and said, "Ladies and gentlemen, it is my privilege to be here today to honor Miss Marji Parker. As you know, she's a great heroine, and all of us acknowledge the splendid work she's been doing in her counseling center on the Lower East Side."

Reporters were busy taking notes, but the rest of the people there—I'd say there must have been about one hundred crowded around—all clapped vigorously. Remembering I was on camera, I tried to stop squinting and look pleasant.

"Hey, Mr. Mayor, what were you and Miss Parker doing behind closed doors? Isn't that unusual after an award ceremony?"

Here it came!

"As most of you know," the mayor started, "Miss Parker is a very religious person, and she has applied her religion in a very practical way to helping people on the Lower East Side. I'm happy to tell you that in my office a few moments ago she prayed a special prayer for me. I guess she thinks even the mayor needs prayer."

Everybody laughed. So far so good.

"She asked God to help me as mayor," he continued. "And of course, with God helping me, New York City shall continue to be the greatest city in the world."

More applause. Then he said, "That is all," and turned to leave.

I started to walk away, too. But just as I did, someone grabbed my arm. Turning, expecting to see a reporter and be faced with questions, I was surprised to find the police commissioner tugging at my arm. He tried to quiet everybody and then said, "Mr. Mayor, ladies and gentlemen, citizens of the world's greatest city, it's my great privilege to give an additional special award to Miss Parker."

Now what?

"As police commissioner of the city of New York it is my distinct honor to award this badge to Miss Parker and officially induct her into the police department of the city of New York."

The applause was deafening, but I felt sick. This was exactly what I didn't want. Those gang members would be in their jail cells watching this on tonight's news. How they would scream that now they had proof whose side I was on! Now what was I going to do?

I started to back away, but the commissioner still had me by the arm. There was no escape. Mom and Dad were beaming proudly. I sure didn't want to embarrass Dad, so I knew I had to go through with it.

So I smiled wanly, while the commissioner pinned the badge on me. Then he waited for my response.

"Thank you, Mr. Commissioner," I said. "I am deeply honored and humbled to be numbered among the most prestigious people of the world, the police department of the city of New York. I shall respect this honor that you have bestowed on me to the best of my ability."

I hardly knew what I was saying, but the words sounded good. I was already thinking that as soon as I got home, I would put the badge away in a bottom drawer. I didn't want to be known as a police officer; I still wanted to be called "preacher lady."

Once again I stepped back, but the commissioner still

had me by the arm. "Since we have inducted a new member into the police department of the city of New York, we certainly don't want to stop there," he said. "So, Miss Parker, we have something else for you. It is not really an award, but it is something extremely important to every police officer. Captain Tilley, would you step forward, please?"

A group of officers standing to one side parted, and someone I assumed to be Captain Tilley walked toward me carrying—oh, no! He had a holster and a gun!

He was all smiles as he put his arms around me and strapped a gun (I found out later it was a .45 automatic pistol) on me with a gun belt. I felt like a cowboy.

I guess my surprise was really showing because Captain Tilley, the commissioner, the mayor, and everybody else were all standing there laughing and clapping. I must have been a funny sight. Here I was, in a print, flowing dress, with a badge on my chest and a gun belt and gun strapped to my waist! Making the best of the situation, I looked at the TV cameras and smiled. But I knew that smile would be going into jail cells later. I had to say something to try to set the record straight. But what?

I really wanted to take off that stupid holster and gun. I didn't need anything like that. I felt bad enough wearing that badge!

"The mayor told you a little bit about me," I started. "I've gone down into the Lower East Side without guns or bullets. But I've gone down there with authority—the authority of God. I've seen Him do what guns and bullets could not do. I've seen Him turn the hearts of junkies and prostitutes around so they have become Christians. I've seen God protect me when I had nothing more in my hand than a Bible. Certainly I don't want to come across to you as a religious fanatic. I understand why our fine policemen must wear badges and carry guns. Some people understand only the power of force. I accept that. I also accept with deep humility this badge and gun. However, I don't think I'll ever need to use them as long as I have God on my side. Please don't feel that I am ungrateful. I am highly honored. I think that all our wonderful police officers should continue to uphold the honor of their badges. Their guns have saved many lives and shall continue to save even more when used properly. But I shall maintain my faith in God, who is my Helper."

I stepped back, and the crowd applauded. I hoped they understood. I certainly would never put policemen down. But I also wanted to leave the testimony that my faith was in God, not in guns.

The crowd started breaking up, and Mom and Dad came rushing to my side. "Oh, Marji, I am so proud of you," Mother said, beaming. "I was especially proud of the way you handled the situation. You gave the honor to God."

I hugged her, saying, "He's the One who deserves it!"

Dad was standing there, practically glowing. "Imagine, my very own daughter, a member of the police department of the city of New York!" he said. "And Marji, that gold badge you're wearing is not just an ordinary badge; they have given you the rank of deputy inspector!"

I glanced down at the badge, fleetingly thinking how pretty it was.

"You know, Marji," Dad went on, "I always had this secret desire to be a policeman. I never imagined that a member of my family would become a police officer. But you did, and I'm so proud!" He squeezed me, then held me at arm's length. "Here, let me look at your gun," he said. "Is it loaded?"

A policeman standing nearby assured us it wasn't. "But Miss Parker," he said, "those bullets in your gun belt are real ones. All you have to do is jerk out the magazine and put them in."

That idea terrified me. The power of this gun and bullets was awesome. Would I ever have to use it? Should I?

He took some bullets out of the belt and flicked a little thing on the side of the gun. "This is the magazine, and this is how you load it," he said, demonstrating.

Several reporters came over to watch. Something told me to learn what he was doing because I suddenly had a sinking feeling that someday I might indeed be forced to use this gun!

The officer placed the bullets in the magazine, pushed it up, handed it to me, and said, "Now all you have to do is pull the trigger!"

Then he must have realized what he had just done. I had a dangerous weapon in my hands, and I really didn't know anything about using it. So he gently took the gun from my hands, pushed a little switch, and the magazine popped out again. "Here, I'd better unload it," he said. "We don't want any shooting around here."

The crowd finally started to break up, and I breathed a sigh of relief that I had gotten through the ceremony without having someone find out about the death threat I faced.

"Why don't we all go out to dinner and have a little celebration?" Dad suggested. "Your mom, Alex and Amilda, and you and me. Okay?"

I really felt as though I ought to get back down to the Lower East Side. I hadn't accomplished anything down there that day. But I rarely saw Mom and Dad, and I knew this was a moment of triumph for them, too—especially Dad—and I didn't want to disappoint them. So I said, "Hey, that sounds like great fun. And I really haven't had much to eat today."

"What's the matter, Amilda? Aren't you taking care of my daughter?" Dad jested.

"Well, if she would just—" Amilda started.

"Oh, Dad, you know she's a wonderful cook," I interrupted, fearing she would say something about the things I had been through the previous night. "If I ate everything she fixed, you wouldn't be able to recognize me."

That seemed to satisfy him, and our conversation turned to other things. Photographers were still taking pictures as we walked down the City Hall steps and got into Dad's waiting limousine. I was happy to see dear Harry, our chauffeur.

Mom and Dad took us to dinner at the World Trade Center. Dad knew the maitre d', who seated us at a window table. As I looked down on the city, it seemed so peaceful from way up there. I wondered whether the mayor remembered his promise to see what he could do to get the gang members released from jail.

I was glad I had taken off the gun belt and gun before we left the car. Amilda had stuffed them into the suitcase she carried and called a purse. I was thinking of that while I was looking out over the city. I even teased her that if we got stopped, she'd be arrested for carrying a weapon without a permit. She didn't look too worried.

After dinner Dad wanted to take us back to our apartment, but I suggested we take the subway instead. I didn't want to keep emphasizing to that neighborhood that I came from a wealthy family. It just made my work that much more difficult.

Dad was still suggesting that I needed a rest and ought to come home with him and Mom when we finally left them and headed for the subway. It was about nine o'clock as we neared our apartment. I remembered thinking it was too late to do anything at the counseling center, and I was contemplating a nice quiet evening of reading, and then a good night's sleep. I sure needed it.

We started up the steps to the door of our apartment house, and I glanced at the burned-out tenement across the street. There, silhouetted in the moonlight, was that sniper, his rifle pointed toward us. I wanted to yell up at him that I was working on getting his brothers out of jail. And I also admit that I was tempted to pull my pistol out of Aunt Amilda's purse and show him a thing or two!

Just as we got to the door, a shot pinged through the darkness. Uncle Alex, a war veteran, knocked Amilda and me down as he tried to shield us.

Amilda began to scream as she grabbed her leg. She'd been hit!

"Quick!" Alex ordered. "We've got to get inside!"

We all started crawling, with Alex practically dragging Amilda into the relative safety of the foyer. When we were all inside, he slammed the door. Amilda was holding her leg. We could see blood oozing between her fingers.

Alex started examining the wound and announced, "It isn't too bad. Just sort of grazed her. Thank God for that."

I looked closely and noticed that her stocking was torn. I dabbed at the wound a few times with my handkerchief, and the bleeding stopped. "I think if we just put some antiseptic and a bandage on it, it should be enough," Uncle Alex said.

Aunt Amilda began praising the Lord for His goodness in sparing her life. We were indeed fortunate. However, I couldn't help but wonder if that bullet was intended for me. Some of those gang members had guns, but didn't aim very well.

"What should we do now?" I asked.

"Do you think we'd better report him to the police?" Alex asked.

"And get that gang member arrested?" I replied. "No way."

"Well, we've got to do something," he returned. "I don't think that was a warning shot. He's shooting to kill! That young man probably figures he has waited long enough. Maybe he decided that if he killed one of us, we'd do something about his buddies. I don't know which of us that bullet was intended for, but it was intended for somebody. If we can't go to the police, then we'll have to take matters into our own hands. We've got to get up there and disarm him before he hurts somebody badly."

"Are you crazy?" I asked, looking at him in total surprise at the idea of trying to disarm the sniper. "How in the world do you think we can do something like that? You can't walk out in the street and point your finger at him. Before you get your hands raised, you'll have a bullet in your heart!"

"I know, Marji," he responded. "Let's just sit here on the steps for a few minutes and think of how we can do this."

"Well, maybe God has already answered our prayers," Amilda said. "Marji, I knew there was some reason God saw to it that you were awarded this gun."

She reached into her purse and pulled out the gun and gun belt. Handing them to me she said, "Let's go get him!"

I laughed, saying, "Aunt Amilda, I've never shot a gun in my whole life. If I pulled the trigger, I'd probably blow my foot off. No, I can't use it."

"You may just have to use it," Uncle Alex warned.

"Uncle Alex, for crying out loud, I'm not about to pull a gun on anybody. I don't believe God sent me down here to kill people."

"I'm not telling you to kill, Marji," he said solemnly. "I'm just saying that when dealing with a gang member who's in a position like that one across the street, you have to deal in guns."

"Well, what do you want me to do?"

"First of all, we need to let him know that we have a gun, too. I want you to open that door and fire five quick shots into the street."

"What?" I yelled. "I might hit somebody!"

"No, you won't," Uncle Alex assured me. "I want you to fire into the door of that burned-out tenement. Nobody's in there. It's been at least six months since that fire."

I nodded numbly, and Alex commanded, "Here, give me that gun. I'll load it for you."

He took the gun and kept turning it over and over, pushing every little button on it, but nothing happened.

"Here, give it to me," I said.

I remembered the switch on the side, pushed it up, and the magazine popped out.

"Are you sure you've never handled guns before?" Uncle Alex asked, a little hurt that I had been able to do what he couldn't. "You handled that like a pro."

"I watched carefully when that policeman demonstrated how to do it. Here. Hand me those bullets."

As Aunt Amilda started to hand them to me, I asked, "How many do you think I should put in?"

"Five," Uncle Alex replied. "Shoot five in quick succession, and I'm sure that sniper will get the message."

I pushed the bullets into the magazine, then pushed the magazine up inside the gun until I heard it click. I curled my fingers around the handle.

"Okay, Marji. I'll open the door slightly," Alex said. "You fire those five shots in quick succession into that door across the street. Then turn and dash up the stairs. The sniper may return the fire and shoot into our door. We can't take the chance of having somebody behind it."

My heart pounded wildly. What if someone were behind that door across the street and I accidentally killed him? That would ruin my ministry! And the police commissioner would get roasted for giving me a gun!

"Uncle Alex, I don't think it's wise to shoot at that door. Suppose somebody just happens to be behind it."

He pooh-poohed the idea with, "Marji, there's nobody behind that door. It's a burned-out tenement!"

"Well, the devil is working against us," I responded. "Maybe he has somebody planted over there behind that door. You know how people sometimes sleep in those places. I'm really afraid someone is over there. I can't shoot at that door. Why don't I just shoot into the pavement?"

"No, don't do that!" Alex warned. "The bullets will ricochet. Then they really might bounce up and hurt somebody."

Then I remembered that the steps of that tenement were cement. "I'll aim for the steps," I said. "If there is any ricochet, it will hit the side of the building."

"Good idea, Marji. But do you think you can hit the steps?"

"Well, I'll do my best. Here goes."

"Amilda, you start up the steps," Alex said. "just in case he opens fire when I swing the door open."

I stretched out on the floor, holding the gun straight out in front of me, ready for Alex to open the door. But then I started trembling so hard that I couldn't hold the gun still. I knew I couldn't hit any steps. I was afraid I wouldn't even be able to hit the side of the building!

Alex saw what was happening and suggested, "Marji, grip with both hands. There will be a little kick to that gun, but not much. But you'll do better with both hands."

I gripped with both hands and, although I still trembled, the gun did seem steadier.

"Okay, I'm going to open that door just a crack," he said. "Then you take aim at those steps and start shooting."

"But Uncle Alex," I protested, "suppose somebody is coming down the street at the exact moment I start shooting. I mean, someone could walk right into the line of fire! Or a car could come by. It's simply not worth that kind of risk!"

"You're getting smarter all the time," Alex told me. "I

should have thought of that. Amilda, you go up to the apartment and check out the street. Be careful, now. The sniper will be watching for any movement inside the apartment. Take a broom and hit the door twice if it's all clear; hit it four times if there's danger. Got it?"

She nodded and trudged up the stairs. I noticed she was favoring that wounded leg slightly. Thank God the wound wasn't any more serious than it was!

I lay there, gun outstretched, hands trembling. This seemed like such a stupid thing to do. What difference did it make whether or not the sniper knew we had a gun? But Uncle Alex usually was savvy about dealing with problems. His idea obviously was better than mine—since I didn't have any.

He opened the door slightly and I tensed, taking aim at the steps and awaiting the signal from Aunt Amilda.

Just then a car drove by. My heart almost stopped. Suppose I had just started shooting when Uncle Alex opened the door. Someone would have been killed! I broke out into a cold sweat.

I thought I heard a thump. Was she hitting with the broom? I would have expected a more definite signal.

As if anticipating my question, Uncle Alex said, "No, that didn't sound like the signal. I think that's just someone walking around."

I wondered what would happen if some of the other tenants came down and found me sprawled out in the foyer aiming a gun into the steps of a burned-out tenement! They'd probably figure I had finally flipped my wig!

But what if some tenant was coming in? Would the sniper be able to distinguish him from us in the darkness? Would he care? Would I be the cause of innocent people being killed?

We waited and waited, hardly daring to move or even breathe. What had happened to Aunt Amilda?

Finally Alex said, "You wait there. I'll go up and

check. I can't figure out what is taking her so long. We should have heard some kind of a signal by now."

Oh, no! I hadn't even thought about what might have happened to her. What if someone was in our apartment? Maybe junkies were in there torturing her! No, she probably still hadn't had the chance to poke her head out the window to see whether or not it was all clear.

Alex took the steps two at a time. I lay there, tense, waiting. But he didn't come back. What could have happened to him? I decided to wait three more minutes. If he didn't come after that time, I was going to find out for myself.

Three minutes ticked by, and still there was no sign of Alex. Nothing. So I headed cautiously up the stairs, the gun in front of me. What had happened to my aunt and uncle? I had an eerie feeling I was going to need the gun.

11

I stopped momentarily before our apartment door, feeling very strange about carrying a gun. Would I have to use it? If it was a showdown between "them" and me, would I be able to pull the trigger? Would God want me to do that? I really didn't know.

I knocked on the door and waited. No answer. This was really spooky. I had seen both my aunt and uncle go up the stairs. I couldn't see the apartment door from where I was lying, but I was reasonably sure they had gone to the apartment. So why didn't someone answer?

I knocked harder. Still no answer. "Uncle Alex, are you in there?" I yelled. "Aunt Amilda, are you in there?" The only sound was my voice echoing in the corridor.

Should I go call the police? But how was I going to get by that sniper? I had to go inside and find out what was going on. At least I had the gun. Maybe if I surprised "them"....

I eased the door open soundlessly and looked around. There were lights on, but I couldn't see anyone anywhere.

I gripped the gun in front of me as I walked into the living room. Then, without thinking, I called, "Uncle Alex, are you here?"

No sooner had I done that than I realized it was a stupid thing to do. If anybody was in the apartment, they'd know now right where I was.

As I walked down the hallway, I heard an almost muffled voice say, "Marji, in here!"

The voice came from my bedroom. With a sense of relief, I pushed the door open. As my eyes became accustomed to the darkness—I didn't flip on the light because of the sniper—my sense of relief was short-lived. There sat Aunt Amilda and Uncle Alex—with knives at their throats. A girl yelled, "Drop that gun, Marji Parker, or you've just seen your aunt and uncle for the last time!"

I opened my hand, and the gun tumbled to the floor. It was then I realized I was staring at two girl members of the Hidden Skulls.

Both were dressed completely in black. Across their chests were a skull and crossbones. Above that, they had sewn a piece of cloth which draped down over the insignia. That's why they were called the Hidden Skulls.

"Okay, what do you two want?"

"Our gang president wants to see you."

This was getting to be a habit. What would the Hidden Skulls want from me? Did they want to thank me for getting all the Tattooed Terrors jailed?

"Okay, I get the message. Now will you just put those knives away?"

"Not that easy," one of them said. "You see, Bonehead is going to stay here while you and I go to headquarters. If our trip is successful, we'll let your aunt and uncle go. But if you try anything, you might as well kiss them good-bye now."

"Now just wait a minute!" I responded. "It isn't all that easy for me, either. Here; let me show you something."

I motioned them toward the window. "What are you trying to do?" Bonehead asked. "We're not about to walk over there. *You* walk over there."

I sure wasn't going to try to pull anything funny—not with those switchblades at the throats of my aunt and uncle! I knew these debs and dolls. They were vicious enough to kill!

As I moved back, Bonehead dropped her knife from Aunt Amilda's neck and grabbed the gun I had dropped, aiming it toward me.

"Easy, Bonehead. That thing is loaded," I said.

"What are you doing with a gun, preacher lady?"

Did I dare tell her about the award? I almost ignored her question, but then I figured I didn't have much to lose.

"You two girls may not believe this," I said, "but we just came back from a ceremony where I was honored by the New York City Police Department. They gave me a badge and a gun."

Both of them laughed. "Listen, I can lie better than that," one of them said. "I know why you carry a gun— for protection."

I wasn't going to press the subject. Getting my aunt and uncle free was far more important.

"Okay, Bonehead," I said. "You've got my gun, so you shouldn't be worried about my trying to pull something. Now will you come over to the window?"

"No tricks?" she asked.

"No tricks," I answered. "But I need you to take a look at something; your plan has its problems."

As she joined me at the window, I said, "Careful; don't get too visible. But look over there on that rooftop across the street, and tell me what you see."

She squinted. Then she began to curse. "Dry Bones," she said to her partner, "you won't believe this, but there's a guy on the roof across the street, sitting there with a rifle pointed over this way."

Just then he let out that bloodcurdling scream again, and Bonehead said, "Hey! That's one of the Tattooed Terrors!"

Dry Bones forgot she was supposed to be guarding my aunt and uncle, and she came running to the window.

Bonehead spun around, pointing the gun at Alex and Amilda. "One move, and I'll blow your brains out!" she threatened.

They sat there as rigid as could be. I believe they were as frightened as I was!

When Dry Bones spotted the sniper, she said, "Bonehead, give me the gun. I think I can pick him off from right here. That way I can avenge the death of Flaming Skull." She turned to me. "He was my boyfriend, but he's dead now. A Tattooed Terror got him. Now I'm going to get a Tattooed Terror!"

As Dry Bones reached for the gun, Bonehead pulled it away. "Hey, man, let's not get into this squabble," she said. "If we don't deliver Marji Parker, we're going to be in big trouble. We came here to deliver her, not to get any Tattooed Terror."

"Did you know that most of the rest of the Tattooed Terrors are in jail?" I asked. "The cops arrested them."

"Yeah, man. We heard about that one," Bonehead said. "That sure was stupid of the Tattooed Terrors to all get in one place and let the cops sneak up on them. We all had a big laugh over that one."

"Well, let me tell you something else," I said. "The Tattooed Terrors think I'm the one who called the cops on them. The reason that sniper is over there is that they have a death threat on my life. A few minutes ago he shot and hit my Aunt Amilda in the leg."

Both of them turned, and Dry Bones pointed.

"You mean that guy actually took a shot at you?"

"Yes, he did," I answered. "I think he was trying to kill me."

"Well, we'll take care of that right now," Dry Bones announced. "Come on, Bonehead. Give me the gun. I have a score to settle."

I knew that if Dry Bones killed that sniper, that would be the end of my immediate problem. But I sure didn't want any killings around here. I knew that young man had an eternal soul that I needed to reach with the Gospel.

"Why don't we work a deal?" I said, trying to deter any bloodshed. "Why don't we just go over there and disarm him and tie him up? The other Tattooed Terrors will, I'm sure, be released soon; the sniper will go back to them as soon as that happens. Then I'm sure that death threat will be taken off me."

"I say we kill him!" Dry Bones exclaimed.

"No. I don't want the cops pinning a murder rap on anybody," I said. "But if we walk out our apartment door, he'll shoot again. Somehow, we're going to have to get that gun away from that sniper, or he is going to get all of us."

"I guess you're right," Bonehead told me. "But do you have any ideas about how we're going to do it?"

"Let me help you out," Uncle Alex offered.

"Mister, what do you think you can do?" Dry Bones asked. "You sound awfully brave."

"I say we take the chance, cross the street, go into that tenement, and surprise him," Alex said. "I've got a plan I used to use in the army. I think it will work, if you co-operate with me."

"Well, I don't see that we have much choice," Bonehead said. "I sure don't want to get knocked off by some Tattooed Terror. That would be utter disgrace for me! But how do we know you're not going to take advantage of us?"

"You have my word," Uncle Alex responded. "After we disarm the fellow, we'll come back here to the apartment and take up where we left off. But in the meantime, you'll have to trust me, just as I'm going to trust you. Our lives depend on that trust. So I promise you again—no funny stuff."

"Well, there had better not be any," Dry Bones said. "Don't forget that we have other gang members. They know we're here. They're waiting for us to bring Marji back. If we don't get back soon, they'll come after us. And they'll stop at nothing!"

The way she said it was enough to strike terror into the heart of the fearless!

"This is what I'm going to do," Uncle Alex started. "I need a gun. Dry Bones, go to my dresser in the other bedroom. Down in the bottom drawer, you'll find a gun. Get it and bring it to me."

I could hear her rummaging around in the other bedroom. Then she returned with the gun.

"All right," Uncle Alex said. "This is where you're going to have to trust me. I promise I won't use it on either of you girls. But you'll have to trust me enough to let me carry it."

I watched Dry Bones, inwardly feeling the tension. Would she do it? No one moved. I waited, breathless.

"Dry Bones, you don't have anything to lose," Alex told her. "If you take a chance on running out into the street while that Tattooed Terror is still on the roof, you'll stand a good chance of getting killed. So trust me. I say we disarm him, and then you can have Marji."

Dry Bones just couldn't bring herself to give a gun to her prisoner. It just didn't make sense. But when Bonehead pointed out that she still had him covered, Dry Bones walked across the room and put the gun in his hands.

"Okay, we'll all go down to the foyer," Alex said. "Amilda will watch and signal us when the street is clear. I'll open the door down there and open fire toward the rooftop. I won't shoot at the sniper, but I want to be sure to aim high enough that I won't hit any innocent bystanders. Anyway, as soon as I open fire, I want the three of you to take off across the street. Then when you three get across, one of you start firing up toward the sniper so I can get across the street. In the army we called that 'covering.' "

"Wow! This is exciting!" Dry Bones exclaimed. "Just like the movies!"

"Come on, let's be serious," Uncle Alex pleaded. "I don't want anyone to get hurt—especially you two girls."

"What did you just say?" Bonehead asked in surprise.

"I said I don't want you two girls to get hurt."

"I just don't understand you people," Dry Bones said. "You could pull that gun on us and kill us, but you don't. I really shouldn't trust you, but something inside of me is making me do it. You people are kind of strange. What is it about you?"

"We're born-again Christians," I said.

"Born-again Christians? What in the world are they?"

"We're people who have given our lives to Jesus. He's changed us and made us new people. We call it being born again."

"Man, if I could be born over again, I'd be born into a rich family. I mean, I'd live like a queen."

"Well, girls, I've got great news for you," Aunt Amilda chimed in. "That's where we're born—into a King's house. And not just any king. We're born into the house of the King of kings!"

"Well, what are you people doing down here on the Lower East Side, then? If you're so rich, you really must be stupid to live down here. If I were this rich, I'd get out of here!"

"Aunt Amilda is talking about Jesus," I said, smiling. "We've been born into His family. He is the King of kings and Lord of lords. And the Bible says when we take Jesus as our Saviour, then we become joint heirs with Jesus. We're in the family of God, the richest family in the world!"

I could sense the girls' growing interest, so I suggested we move out of the darkness of my bedroom into the living room. As we walked out there, Bonehead said,

"You're not putting us on, are you?"

I laughed. "No, girls, what I'm telling you is really the truth. You can have a completely new life-style if you're born again."

"Well, I have news for you," Bonehead remarked. "I was born in poverty, and I'll die in poverty. There's no way out for me now. I became a gang member for my own protection. They told me they would kill me out on the streets unless I joined up, so I joined to stay alive. I mean, I had no choice!"

"Well, Bonehead," I said, "you have a choice now. You can choose either life or death. You can choose freedom or bondage. You can choose heaven or hell. And you can choose Jesus rather than Satan."

"Hey, let's get off this religious kick," Dry Bones said disgustedly. "We've got work to do."

"You know, girls," I said, ignoring the interruption, "it's never too late to give your heart to Jesus. No matter what you have done or how bad you think you are, He still wants to give you the peace and life that only He can bring."

"Oh, that's nice for people like you," Bonehead protested. "But it's not for the likes of us."

"Oh, but it is," I corrected. "Have you ever heard of Nicky Cruz, head of the Mau Mau gang in Brooklyn?"

"No. We never get to Brooklyn. We have enough action around here."

"Well, Nicky Cruz was a gang leader for a number of years. He's been where you girls are; his gang had its debs and dolls, too. They had their fights and murders and all the rest. But one day Nicky came across a preacher by the name of David Wilkerson. And through that encounter, Nicky eventually gave his heart and life to Jesus. Today he himself is an evangelist and is winning many people to Jesus. He's a well-respected man. Now if Jesus can do something like that for Nicky Cruz, girls, He can do it for you, too."

"You mean the president of the Mau Maus got religion?" Bonehead asked in surprise. "You must be crazy."

"No, I'm not crazy," I responded. "It's the truth. In fact, some of the other gang members became Christians, too—including the vice-president of the gang."

They both looked at me unbelievingly—and hungrily.

"I tell you, girls, when Jesus comes into your life, a revolution takes place," I went on. "It's a revolution for good. You suddenly become aware of what life is all about. Life becomes a challenge—not the challenge to kill the Tattooed Terrors, but a challenge to become whatever the Lord has in mind for your life.

"And another beautiful thing happens. Instead of wanting to hurt people, you now want to help people. That's what happened to me. I really don't have time to go into all of my past, but I've come from the other side of the fence. I was born and raised in wealth, on a beautiful estate out on Long Island. But when I was in college, I learned I was a sinner. I asked Jesus to save me. He became very real to me. After college, I started working in my dad's company. I could have been on easy street for the rest of my life. But I wasn't satisfied with that kind of life. I knew Jesus had more important things for me to do. He led me to come down here and open my counseling center to try to help the people in the Lower East Side. I'm not doing this out of any thought of a reward. I'm doing it because Jesus' love within me makes me want to do all I can to help other people."

The girls were silent, listening intently to what I said. I guess they'd never come across anyone quite like me before. I even noticed that Bonehead had dropped the gun to her side—no longer did she have it trained right on me. I knew the Holy Spirit was grabbing her heart, convicting her of her sin and of her need for a Saviour.

"You know, girls, it's not necessary to be in a church

to receive Jesus as your Saviour. That miracle can occur right here. As soon as you ask Him, He'll forgive your sin and give you a peace and joy you've never experienced before."

Alex and Amilda were silently praying. They sensed what I sensed—that at least one of these girls was right now in the throes of a decision.

"You need His peace to stop the wars going on inside your heart," I urged. "Wouldn't you like to receive Jesus right now?"

Both of them stood there, still silent. Did I note tears glistening in their eyes? Were they beginning to see that there was hope for them through Jesus? I knew the Holy Spirit was doing the work Jesus said He had come to this world to do. They never had thought any hope existed for them. It was taking time for the truth to sink in through all that unbelief and hardness.

"Listen, girls, why don't we make an altar of God right here?" I asked. "This room can be His altar. If you'll just kneel with us right now and receive Jesus into your hearts, I'll guarantee that things will be different for you."

"Okay, suppose we do that," Bonehead said. "What about our mission? We've got to deliver you to the gang, Marji, or they're going to kill us."

"I'll tell you what, girls," I responded. "As soon as you receive Jesus and we can figure a way around that sniper, I'll go willingly with you. Uncle Alex and Aunt Amilda will go, too, if you wish. We'll all go. We'll march into that headquarters and have a revival! We'll tell all of them about Jesus and share with them the great experience the two of you have had being born again. You'll be absolutely amazed at what God can do through your testimony. In fact, if you receive Jesus here tonight, that could be what God uses to bring a great revival to the Lower East Side. It might even put an end to these senseless gang wars and murders!"

The more I talked, the more excited I got. It seemed as though God was showing us this was His way of starting a series of miracles down here. And it would start by these girls' becoming born-again Christians.

"Girls, the choice is yours," I said, pressing the claims of Christ upon them. "If I could, I would kneel down and receive Jesus for you. But I can't do that. God has given each person a free will. So it's entirely a personal decision. Wouldn't you like to receive Him?"

Dry Bones looked over at Bonehead, and Bonehead looked at me. I noticed it was a pleading look—a look that said, "Oh, how I wish what you are saying was true."

I waited, sensing this was the time to let the Holy Spirit speak to their hearts in a way I couldn't. I knew the kind of battle that was going on within them. But the Holy Spirit also witnessed to my heart that Jesus would win the victory.

Bonehead looked over at Dry Bones and said, "What do you think, kid?"

"Dry Bones, it's a decision you'll never be sorry for," I said.

Dry Bones turned the toe of her shoe into the almost threadbare carpet on the floor. "Okay," she finally said. "I'll try it once. But if it doesn't work, I'll never try it again!"

"Let's kneel right here," I said. "I know Jesus wants to do something special for both of you."

The five of us knelt in a circle. I positioned myself between Dry Bones and Bonehead, putting my arms around them.

"Now, girls, it's not difficult to receive Jesus," I assured them. "People sometimes try to make it difficult, but it's so simple that even little children can understand. There are three things you have to do."

They both looked at me eagerly.

"Number one is to acknowledge that you're a sinner.

Now you girls have sinned, haven't you?"

They both laughed at the obvious answer to that question. "Are you kidding?" Bonehead asked. "Probably a thousand times."

"I think I sin two thousand times a day!" Dry Bones chimed in. "I mean, I'm really bad news."

"Well, the Bible agrees with that," I said. "It tells us that we all have sinned and come short of the glory of God. That means I have sinned; Uncle Alex and Aunt Amilda have sinned; Bonehead, you've sinned; Dry Bones, you've sinned. That makes us all sinners, doesn't it?"

The girls smiled. They could readily see the logic of it. And I found it surprisingly easy to identify with these girls. We were all sinners. The only difference was that three of us had already asked Jesus to forgive our sins.

"The second thing is to ask Jesus to forgive your sins," I went on. "For some people, that can be very difficult. They think they have been the worst sinners in the world—for example, murderers. How could Christ forgive a murderer, they wonder. Well, He does. As far as God is concerned, any sin will send a person to hell. It doesn't matter whether you've been a murderer, a junkie, a prostitute, a gang member, or even a good person who has committed the sin of not believing in the Saviour God sent—everybody needs to have their sins forgiven. So what we are going to do now is to ask Jesus to forgive our sins. It's not necessary to name them one by one. He knows them all. We can just ask Him to forgive all of them."

"But Marji, you've no idea what nasty, evil things I've done," Bonehead interjected, tears glistening on her cheeks. "I mean, I've been a terrible sinner. I am dirty and filthy and wretched. God may be able to forgive some of my sins, but there are other ones so terrible I'd be ashamed for anybody to know about them. I don't see how He could possibly forgive—"

"Bonehead, you don't need to worry about what you've done," I reassured her. "The blood Jesus shed on the cross is powerful enough to cover every sin of every sinner in the whole world! And I mean every single one of them!"

"Hey, this is getting better all the time!" Bonehead exclaimed. "I really need my sins forgiven. They've become such a heavy load!"

"Well, the third thing," I said, "is just by faith to receive Jesus into your heart. What that means is that we believe what He said, and we accept His Word for it. We aren't saved because we happen to feel saved; we are saved because He said that if we confessed our sins and asked Him to forgive us, He'd do it."

I turned to Uncle Alex and said, "Uncle, would you please get your Bible and read Romans, chapter ten, verses nine and ten to these girls? Maybe that will help them."

Alex quickly got up, picked up his Bible from a nearby table, thumbed through the New Testament until he came to the Book of Romans, and knelt back down and read: " 'If thou shalt confess with thy mouth the Lord Jesus, and shalt believe in thine heart that God hath raised him from the dead, thou shalt be saved. For with the heart man believeth unto righteousness; and with the mouth confession is made unto salvation.' "

I looked over at Aunt Amilda. Her eyes were closed, and her lips were moving in a silent prayer. I knew she was claiming two trophies for God's kingdom!

"Girls, just repeat this prayer after me," I said.

"Lord Jesus, I know I'm a sinner. Please forgive me. Please forgive me of all my sins."

I paused after each phrase, and the girls repeated the prayer.

"And Lord Jesus, thank You for forgiving all my sins," I went on. "By faith I receive You into my heart. Amen."

They both prayed the words, but after the "Amen," Dry Bones said, "I don't feel any different."

I remembered she had said she'd try it once, so I prayed to the Lord to give me wisdom in answering her.

"Dry Bones," I said, "do you remember what I said about faith? At this point, feelings have nothing to do with it. We accept it as true because Jesus said it was true."

She looked a little puzzled, so I said, "According to that prayer we just prayed, where is Jesus right now?"

Her forehead contorted as she thought about what she had just prayed. Then she brightened. "I asked Him into my heart," she said. "That means He's in my heart right now!"

"That's it! That's it!" I said excitedly. "Christ is in your heart. When you invited Him in, He came in. And your believing that He did what He said He would do is what we call faith. It really doesn't make any difference how you feel about it. He really did come into your heart, and He'll always be there, as long as you want Him to be."

"You mean it's that easy?" Bonehead asked. "You mean that's all we have to do?"

"That's all you have to do to be born again," I answered. "But now you're just like a newborn baby. You've taken the first step, and you've entered God's kingdom. But the second step is to grow. You learn that by studying God's Word—the Bible—and finding a good church to worship together with other Christians. The Lord will teach you how to live according to His Word. He's got many beautiful principles of life that He'll teach you from the Bible. I have a Bible study every Wednesday evening at the counseling center. A lot of people from the street attend. I want you two to come and join us. That will be one way you'll learn to grow as Christians."

"But what about our gang members?" Dry Bones

asked anxiously. "They'll never let us go free. They'll kill us if we try to get out!"

"Yes, that's right!" Bonehead chimed in. "I remember that two years ago a girl tried to split. Her parents threatened to send her away upstate. The next day our president and vice-president had to kill her."

I knew these gangs meant business. They didn't tolerate any defections. But I also knew that God was more powerful than any New York City gang!

"Girls, let me assure you that God is able to take care of you," I said. "He's saved you, and He's done it for a purpose. I believe this is the beginning of the great revival we have been praying for. What God did for Nicky Cruz and some of the members of the Mau Maus, He can do for you and the Hidden Skulls. The Bible says that nothing is impossible with God, and I believe it!"

"Well, man, I sure don't want to die," Dry Bones said. "I'm not ready to die."

I smiled. "Oh, but you are, Dry Bones. Now you're really ready to die. Jesus has given you eternal life. If something were to happen to you this very minute and your earthly life ended, you'd be right in heaven! There you'd live with the Saviour forever and ever! I know what you mean, Bonehead—you're not *anxious* to die. But you really are *ready* to die now!"

I could tell that what Jesus had done in their lives was beginning to sink in. I didn't know how everything was going to work out, but somehow I knew it was. God's working was indeed evident!

As we were on our knees in the circle, talking more about the new life in Christ, suddenly we heard the report of a rifle and the smashing of glass in my bedroom. That sniper must have seen the lights on elsewhere in the apartment and was reminding us he was still up there!

Dry Bones started to curse. I almost rebuked her gently because Christians aren't supposed to swear, but I remembered that she had been a Christian only a few minutes. She had a lot of growing to do.

"Let's go get that guy!" Dry Bones exclaimed. "We can't let him get by with that sort of nonsense. I mean, let's go right now and knock him off!"

"Now wait a minute," I cautioned. "We agreed that we would try to disarm him. But remember, we're all Christians now. We're not going to kill him."

Another shot rang out, and more glass smashed. Dry Bones cursed again.

"Dry Bones," I said, "God has washed your heart clean. Now you need to let Him clean up your tongue, too. Please don't swear anymore."

She laughed. "Okay, I hear you."

We all got up from our knees and stood around as Uncle Alex went through the plan again. Bonehead walked over and handed my gun back to me. "You'd better carry it," she said. "I might be tempted to use it on that guy."

"Thanks for your trust," I responded. "We'll simply try to disarm the sniper. I don't think God will let us get killed."

"Well," Uncle Alex said, "if any of us do get killed, there's one thing for sure: we'll meet in heaven."

As we opened the apartment door to go down the steps to the foyer, I wondered about what he had just said. Was he prophesying that one of us was going to die?

12

As we walked down the steps, Bonehead said, "Hey, why don't we just forget this whole thing? I mean, Dry Bones and I got saved, so let's forget the whole thing with this sniper. Okay?"

I didn't say so aloud, but I had to agree that it did seem stupid to try to disarm that sniper.

"To tell you the truth," Uncle Alex said, as we all congregated in the foyer, "I would just as soon go upstairs and go to bed and forget this thing, too. But if we don't get that sniper, he's going to get somebody. If you go out in the street and yell for him to put his gun down, he'll kill you. Why, if you even try to sneak out that door, he'll probably kill you. We've got to get to him, and I believe God is going to help us."

"Well, I'll tell you something," Dry Bones said. "We'll take that sniper, but that's it. I'm not going any further. I want to get out of this city quickly. And I'm not going back to my gang, either! They'll kill me!"

"Now come on, Dry Bones," I said softly. "This is the time to trust God. So let's do first things first. We'll disarm the sniper first. Then we'll pray about whether or not we ought to go back to the headquarters of the Hidden Skulls. You know, the Bible tells about how Jesus went to His own people. The Apostle Paul went to his own people. And I really believe God will help us if He wants you to go to your own people. Uncle Alex and I will go with you, okay?"

"You people are nuts, I mean, really nuts!" Dry Bones exclaimed. "If you were in the gangs the way I was, you'd understand. I mean, once you try to get out of the gang, it's all over. And knowing them and what they think about you, they're not only going to kill us; they're going to kill you, too. Who do you people think you are, anyway?"

"Hey, hold on there, Dry Bones," Bonehead cut in. "You sound as though you're chicken already. What's the matter? Are you afraid?"

"Of course I'm afraid!" she exploded. "I suppose you're going to stand there and try to tell me you're not afraid!"

"I didn't say that," Bonehead answered. "But don't you remember what Marji said? We have faith. We put our faith to work. I can't understand you, Dry Bones. You're usually the first one who's ready to go out on the streets and kill someone. Now all of a sudden you change. I ought to rap you in the head. That's what I ought to do!"

Dry Bones doubled her fist, so I stepped between them and said, "Hey, girls, let's cool it! You've got to ask the Lord to take all this quarreling out of your heart. If you're going to fight, let's fight the devil, not each other."

Dry Bones relaxed and said, "Come on. Let's get this over with. I'll feel a lot better when we take care of that sniper. At least I can go back and tell the gang I disarmed a member of the Tattooed Terrors!"

"I wouldn't mention it," Bonehead warned. "They'll want to know why you didn't kill him."

At that, Uncle Alex said, a little anxiously, "Remember now, only disarming—no killing!"

I glanced at Dry Bones. The look in her eyes was telling me a lot. Would she stop at disarming? I knew she hated the Tattooed Terrors with a vengeance. Given a standoff, she'd probably shoot to kill.

"Okay, so we all get across the street, then what?" Bonehead asked.

"Well, we'll do what we used to do in the army," Uncle Alex replied. "We went forward by retreating."

Dry Bones screamed, "Man, I just can't understand what you're talking about! There's no way I'm going to retreat before a Tattooed Terror! No way!"

"Now hold on a minute and let me explain," Alex said. "You've got to stay cool under fire. If you lose your cool, you're going to lose your life!"

He let that sink in. Then he went on: "We'll blaze away so we can all get across the street by covering each other. Once we're across the street, we'll go up into the tenement. When we get to the floor next to the roof, you two girls will start screaming, hissing, and taunting him. When he chases you, you retreat—you run. But when he comes down those stairs after you, Marji and I will be hidden and get him when he comes by. It's as simple as that."

"Sounds too simple," Dry Bones responded.

"That's just it," Alex replied. "The simpler it is, the easier it is to pull off. There's only one thing. You've got to do something to make sure that sniper wants to get at you."

"No problem," Dry Bones announced. "All I have to do is call him a bunch of dirty names."

"No! No! No!" I interrupted. "Remember that God has cleaned up your heart and wants to clean up your tongue! No cursing or swearing or dirty words!"

Bonehead laughed. "Marji, I tell you this business of getting saved sure makes it hard to be a gang member!"

"That's the whole point," I replied. "Christ wants you in His army—not in a gang. He wants you to fight against evil, not other people. He wants you to bring peace, not destruction."

I guess I was getting carried away, because Bonehead laughingly said, "Marji, I think all we need to do is have you run out there in that street with a beautiful bunch of flowers. I'm sure that sniper will lay his rifle down when he sees that!"

We all laughed, and it helped relieve the tension of the moment. I knew there were times God wanted us to bring flowers—after all, He created them for our enjoyment. But I didn't think that was His plan for this minute! I felt reassured that God knew our motives, and I was hoping we'd be able to pull this thing off without having anyone get hurt.

"Everybody ready?" Uncle Alex asked.

We three girls crouched at the door, ready to run. "I'll open the door," Alex explained. "But don't run until I fire."

My leg muscles tightened so hard they almost cramped. Then Alex jerked the door open wide and started firing up at the upper floor of the burned-out tenement. The noise was deafening!

At the first shot, Dry Bones was out the door. Bonehead was on her heels. I'd never seen girls run so fast in all my life. I was a distant third.

Uncle Alex was still firing away when we slammed, panting, against the building where the sniper was holed up. Now it was my turn to provide cover fire for Uncle Alex. I was shaking from head to foot, gripping the gun as hard as I could. But I had it pointed down, toward the sidewalk.

"Marji, for crying out loud, open fire!" Dry Bones screamed.

I glanced and saw Uncle Alex crouched in the street—an open target for the sniper! He, too, was yelling for me to fire. But I just couldn't!

Bonehead leaped to my side, grabbed my arm, and raised it so the gun was pointing straight up. "Pull the trigger!" she screamed in my ear. "Pull the trigger!"

I gripped as hard as I could. Finally, the gun went off. The recoil jerked my arm, so I grabbed that arm with the other hand and held on tight. Then I squeezed the trigger again and again. Bullets went zinging into the air.

At the first shot, Alex started across the street, his own gun held high and blazing away. When he slammed safely against the wall next to us, he ordered, "Okay, everybody inside. Quickly!"

We jumped to the doorway, breathless from the excitement—especially me. I made a mental note that I was going to have to get more physical exercise. I was getting out of shape.

We regrouped inside the tenement door. "Whew! That was close!" Uncle Alex exclaimed. "When you didn't open fire right away, Marji, I thought I was a dead duck!"

"Sorry," I said lamely. "I guess I lost my cool. Bonehead was the one who got me straightened out." Then I asked, "Did you see the sniper?"

"Only his gun. He was too smart to poke his head over when our guns were blazing. I don't know if he realizes we're in the same building he is, but he's sure going to find out!"

Alex sounded as if he almost relished this whole mess!

The spooky darkness of the hallways made me shudder as we let our eyes get accustomed to the lack of light. We felt our way to the stairs, stopped, and peered up. We couldn't see very far, and I said, "What if, while we're walking up these stairs to get to him, he's walking down to see what we're doing? Suppose he surprises us?"

"Yes. Marji's right," Bonehead whispered. "That Tattooed Terror isn't stupid. He knows all about gang warfare. He knows the best method is surprise, and he'll be edgy with all that gunfire."

"That's the chance we'll have to take," Alex replied.

"Somebody has to go first up those stairs, and it isn't going to be me!" Dry Bones announced. Then she looked over at me and said, "You're a Christian, aren't you?"

I nodded, but I wondered what she was getting at.

"Well, since you're a real Christian and believe God will protect you, I think you should lead the way up the stairs."

"Now wait a minute!" I responded. "Just because I'm a Christian doesn't mean that—"

"Ha!" Dry Bones responded sarcastically. "I was wondering about this Christianity. I guess it doesn't really work when you face danger, does it?"

Something inside of me exploded, and I ordered, "Okay, you people, follow me!" With that, I started up the stairs. Alex moved alongside me, and Dry Bones was directly behind us. "Okay, Marji, I'm convinced," she replied. "But use your head. Go quietly!"

I got on my tiptoes, but those old stairs still creaked and groaned. It was going to be difficult to sneak up on that sniper.

"Marji, that was probably the first time you shot a gun out there on the street," Dry Bones whispered. "Good thing you weren't shooting to kill, because you couldn't hit the broad side of a tenement building. So while we're walking up the steps, would you do me a favor? Put the gun straight out in front of you. Pretend you're holding it on somebody. If he surprises us and opens fire, it's either him or us. But it's only one of him and four of us! So you'd better start squeezing that trigger right away if he comes into view!"

Then I remembered something. "Hey, wait a minute!" I said, stopping everybody. "I almost did something stupid!"

I handed the gun to Uncle Alex, who asked me, "What's the matter? Aren't you going to use it?"

I replied sheepishly, "Remember how you used to count the shots in the Westerns on TV? Did you count my shots? I don't think there are any bullets left in that gun."

Bonehead cursed. "You're really stupid, Marji!"

I wanted to scream at her to stop picking on me, but I controlled my temper and whispered, "Hey, don't call me stupid. You girls are supposed to be gang fighters, and you didn't remember, either."

"Now, now, let's keep everything Christian," Uncle Alex said calmly.

A moment later, I realized why he had said it so calmly. First he reloaded my gun. Then he announced lamely, "I forgot to reload mine, too."

"The great war hero!" Dry Bones said sarcastically. "Wouldn't it have looked great if we had met that sniper in a shoot-out, and both your guns simply went *click, click, click?*"

As I watched Alex reloading his gun, I realized that what we were doing just didn't add up. Christians didn't go around with loaded guns, trying to disarm gang members. But we had gone too far to turn back now. Besides, we'd never be able to get back into our apartment building. We did have to try to disarm the sniper.

When we got the guns loaded, we headed toward the second floor. All of us were on tiptoe, but still the stairs were creaking like crazy. If the sniper was inside, surely he could hear us coming!

As we got to the second floor, I noticed a dim light coming from under a door just off the stairs. Strange. Then I heard something crash. All of us jumped back. Had the sniper set up an ambush for us? Was he trying to lure us into that room?

I pointed the gun at the door, but Uncle Alex motioned us all onto the floor.

"What should we do now?" I asked.

"Well, I can either fire through that door, or he'll open fire on us," Alex said. "I think we—"

"No! No!" I interrupted. "We can't afford to do that! Remember what we said? We said we would disarm him, not kill him."

"I know! I know!" Alex responded. "Marji, I'm not in

the killing business. I'll fire above the door."

"But suppose that isn't the sniper in there!" I exclaimed. "I mean, you know as well as I do that all kinds of people stay in these abandoned tenements. It could be a junkie; it could be a prostitute. It could be a mother on welfare with her two kids."

"Okay, we'd better not shoot," Alex agreed. "So here's what I'll do. I'll jump up and crash the door in. As soon as I do, I'll leap to the side. If it's the sniper and he opens fire, we'll all start firing to scare him off."

This was absolutely stupid. It sounded like a plot from a cheap movie. Here I was, on the floor with a gun in my hand. Was this what a Christian worker was supposed to do? Why wasn't I back in my counseling center with a Bible in my hand? I sure felt a lot more comfortable in that role!

Uncle Alex eased to his feet and whispered, "Okay? Is everybody ready?"

He looked at me. "Marji, get that gun out in front of you. Put both hands on it."

I did as he instructed, all the while hoping nobody was inside the room. But why would there be a dim light?

Uncle Alex poised. Then with a hard thrust, he hit the door. It went crashing, and I could see him leap to the side.

We waited. No shots. Not a sound.

Then a girl's voice called, "Who's there?"

I started to get up, but Bonehead pushed me down with a whispered, "Stay down! It could be a trap!"

"This is Angie Gorman," Bonehead called back. "I'm looking for my sister Barbara. Have you seen her?"

That Bonehead! The Lord had a lot to do in her heart! But I kept reminding myself that I couldn't expect everything from her immediately. The Bible says we grow and mature as Christians. At this point, she really didn't know any better than to lie. And this was hardly the time or place to explain!

I heard footsteps. Then I saw a girl carrying a candle coming to the door. When she saw us, she demanded, "What in the world is going on here?"

"There's a sniper on the rooftop," Uncle Alex explained. "We are going up to get him."

"Oh. I thought you people were cops or something. They ought to call the cops on that guy. I can't figure him out."

She looked at Bonehead and Dry Bones as we all got up. "Oh. Members of the gangs, huh?"

"Well, yes and no," Bonehead said. "We used to be. But now Marji Parker has enlisted us in the army of the Lord—or something like that."

I laughed and then explained, "You see, we're Christians. We're going up to disarm the sniper on the roof."

"You're Christians?" the girl asked in disbelief, "and you're going up to disarm that sniper? Well, I never. . . ."

I felt my cheeks flush with embarrassment. What we were doing did seem stupid. She probably thought we were escapees from some mental institution!

"You see, he's a member of the Tattooed Terrors, and he's out to get us," I went on lamely.

"You mean the Tattooed Terrors don't like Christians? That gang member is out to kill all Christians?"

This would be difficult to explain. I thought I'd better change the subject. So I asked, "What's your name?"

"Cecelia Hayden."

As soon as she said "Cecelia," bells went off in my brain. Where had I heard that name before? Then it hit me. That was the name of the girl Benny Barnes and Cobra were fighting about. This couldn't possibly be that Cecelia, could it?

"You wouldn't happen to know a couple of pimps

named Benny Barnes and Cobra, would you?"

She jumped back, startled, and pleaded, "Please! Please! Please leave me alone! You haven't come to take me back to them, have you?"

"All I asked was whether you are that Cecelia," I said.

"I guess so," she said. "I've worked for both of them. But the other night I just couldn't take it anymore. Those two monsters are the meanest dudes around. Cobra beat me mercilessly when I didn't bring in as much money as he thought I should. And Benny wasn't much better. I had to get away."

Oh, how my heart went out to that poor girl. She was so skinny and frail. She looked like a junkie. That meant she was supporting her pimp and her drug habit through prostitution. She looked so tired, so weak—as though a strong breeze would blow her down. How I wished that young girls lured by the city would be able to see the end result. Maybe it would scare them away from a life that became a living hell.

"I believe God brought me over here to help you," I said quietly.

She smiled faintly, but suddenly she acted as though something was wrong. She doubled over and heaved, her vomit splattering all over the floor. "I'm sorry," she apologized. "Please excuse me. I'm kicking it, and I'm really sick."

I'd seen this so many times before. Junkies who stop taking dope go through withdrawal. Sometimes they'll try to kick it cold so they can get a quicker high without using so much dope. But if they think they're going to quit and don't have Jesus living in them, they go right back on the needle.

"Will you help me?" she asked pleadingly.

"We sure will!"

"Could you give me ten bucks so I can get a bag and get off? I've got to get straight. I just can't take this kicking."

"Cecelia," I said, "I've got something far better than that. I've got Someone who will more than satisfy that habit of yours."

"You do?" she replied. "You have methadone?"

"Far better than that. I don't know whether you're ready to accept this now or not, but I've been able to help many girls like you. Girls who have been prostitutes and junkies have come to know Jesus Christ as their Saviour. They have been set free from drugs and sin and now they're living beautiful, purposeful lives."

"Oh, come on. Don't string me along. There's no hope like that for me."

"Wrong, Cecelia. God has helped me save a couple of Benny Barnes's girls. I was able to rescue Patti and Suzie. They went upstate to the Walter Hoving Home. They graduated from that program and now both of them are in Bible school. They have been completely changed—delivered from drugs and prostitution—by the power of Christ!"

Cecelia started to leave the hallway and go back inside the room. I gently took her arm and said, "Don't walk away. I really believe we're here tonight by a divine design. We thought we were coming up to disarm a sniper. But God knew you were over here suffering and needing help. I believe He sent us over to help you."

"I must be dreaming," she said. "There's no hope for me."

"There's got to be hope for you, Cecelia," I countered. "We had no idea anyone was in this place. But God knew. He saw how you were hurting, and He arranged the situation so we would come over here. We've come, Cecelia, as God's messengers. He's sent us to tell you He cares about you and can deliver you from the habits and the sins that bind you. If you'll just hang on a few minutes, we'll come back and get you and make arrangements for you to go to the Walter Hoving Home, too. It's up in Garrison, New York. You'll find people up there who really care about you. You'll be safe from the pimps there. And those people will give you a nice warm bed and feed you well."

"I haven't had a decent meal in weeks!" she cried. "And I've been sleeping on the floor here in total terror of rats and who knows what else." Her eyes brimmed with tears.

"I know, Cecelia. I know," I said comfortingly. "That's why I want to get you out of this mess. Those people up at the Walter Hoving Home will teach you what life is all about and how to really live by learning the principles of God's Word. In fact, I think Dry Bones and Bonehead here ought to head up that way, too, to get them away from the gang members who might try to kill them. It's a beautiful home for all girls who need help."

"I need help," Cecelia admitted. "That place sounds almost too good to be true. But I don't have any money to go there."

"Don't worry about it. Christian people all over the United States send money to help support the program. All it will cost you is a willingness to do your best."

"A warm bed and good food?" she asked again.

"All that, and a whole lot more."

"What have I got to lose? When can we go?"

"Well, Cecelia, first we've got to disarm that sniper."

"Can I help you do that?"

"Does he know you live here?" Alex asked.

"Yes," Cecelia answered. "He came down earlier today and demanded food. I had to sneak out and get him some. I was too sick to eat. So he knows I'm here."

"Good!" Alex responded. "Maybe we can set him up and drop him down here."

"Man, that's a great idea!" Bonehead added. "Cecelia, you go up and invite him down to your apartment. Tell him you've got a delicious dinner all fixed for him. He'll come."

"No! No!" I interrupted. "Let's not tell any lies. God would not be honored in that. We'll have to think of something else."

"But getting him down here would be a good idea," Dry Bones said.

We all agreed that it would. Then Cecelia said, "Look, it won't be a problem to get him down here. I have ways."

I knew she was a prostitute, but she certainly wouldn't entice him, would she? I decided not to ask.

"All right," Alex said, "we'll all get inside the apartment. As soon as he comes to the door, we'll get the drop on him. And Cecelia, be careful, won't you?"

She smiled. "I still think I'm dreaming," she said, "and I want to be sure this is a good dream. I'll bring him."

With that, she started up the stairs toward the roof. The four of us took the candle and went into her apartment. As we looked around, we saw the broken window, the gaping holes in the walls, and the pile of rags over in the corner—probably where she slept. I squeezed the loaf of bread sitting on a beat-up old box. It was hard and dry, but it probably was all she had to eat. No wonder that talk of food and bed had intrigued her.

I wondered how a beautiful girl like Cecelia once must have been could end up in filth like this? America was supposed to be the land of opportunity, but here was a scared little girl, fleeing for her life from two evil pimps who had enslaved her, hardly daring to show her face on the street, trying to kick a drug habit that was destroying her.

We had found Cecelia. She was ready to let us help her. But how many thousands of others were there whom no one had been able to reach yet?

"Everybody up close against the wall," Uncle Alex ordered, bringing me back to the danger of the moment. "Let's hope this works."

I was on one side of the door with Bonehead. Alex and Dry Bones were on the other side.

"As soon as you hear steps, Marji, point your gun at the door," Alex instructed. "Don't fire. Just aim. When he comes in, I'll jump him and try to disarm him. When I do that, Bonehead and Dry Bones, you jump, too. The first thing we have to do is get his rifle away. Then we'll pin him. Marji, you keep us covered."

My mind was whirring. Suppose the sniper broke loose and pointed his rifle at me. Would I pull the trigger? Would I go down shooting at him, or would he go down shooting at me? I hated to even contemplate the options!

We waited what seemed like an eternity. What had happened to Cecelia? Had the sniper outsmarted her? Had he taken her hostage? Why didn't she come back?

Then we heard footsteps descending slowly. Uncle Alex blew out the candle. He whispered to me to have my gun pointed at the door. In the tension, I could sense him crouched, ready to spring.

Someone was nearing the door. I held the gun straight out in both hands, one finger on the trigger.

Every muscle in my body tightened as the door creaked open.

13

My heart beat wildly as I tightened my grip on the gun. This was it!

As the door opened and a dark shadow entered, I saw Uncle Alex leap. Bonehead and Dry Bones tackled the shadow, and everybody went sprawling. Oh, if there were only a light I could flip on to see what was happening. I just did as I was told and kept the gun aimed in the general direction where the noise was coming from.

Then a woman's scream pierced the air. Cecelia, from her position flat on the floor, was yelling, "It's me! It's me! I'm alone! Don't shoot! Don't shoot!"

The three of them rolled off her, and Uncle Alex lighted the candle. We all stood there, shaking.

"Did we hurt you, Cecelia?" Bonehead asked.

"Not too badly," she replied, rubbing her stomach. "But one of you sure has a hard right to the stomach."

"That's mine," Bonehead replied. "That tactic makes them bend over. Then you hit them in the back of the head with a strong rabbit punch. Then, baby, it's all over."

"Well, I'm glad we didn't get to that point," Cecelia said. "And thanks, Marji, for not pulling that trigger."

"I couldn't see who was who," I explained. "But I sure wish it had been the sniper. Then it would have been all over. But what happened? How come you didn't bring him down?"

"So help me, I tried everything," Cecelia said. "I

mean, I even hugged and kissed him. I tried with promises of food and a few other things. But he wouldn't budge from up there."

Now we were stuck. We were going to have to go up after him.

"I did learn a few things, though," Cecelia went on. "He is out to kill. And Marji, he is out to kill you. He thinks that setup was your doing. Of course, I didn't tell him you were down here. But I don't believe I've ever seen anybody so angry."

"Come on," Uncle Alex urged. "Let's go get him. I believe the Lord will deliver him into our hands."

As we headed for the hallway, I said to Cecelia, "Stay here. I'm hoping and praying and believing we'll be back soon. I want to take you over to my aunt's apartment. You can stay there while we go to the headquarters of the Hidden Skulls. Then when we get through there, I'll arrange to send you and Bonehead and Dry Bones up to the Walter Hoving Home. God's got a beautiful plan for your life, Cecelia, and you can begin to find it up there."

"I just can't believe it," Cecelia said. "I just can't believe that anyone cares what happens to me!"

"I know how you feel," Bonehead said. "But I probably won't live to see that place up in the country."

Dry Bones slapped her buddy on the back and said, "Come on, Bonehead. We've come this far. We're on God's side now, and I'm really getting the feeling that He's right here with us. Let's finish the job so all three of us can get to that place out in the country. Everything's going to be okay!"

I smiled inwardly at that beautiful expression of faith from one only minutes old in the Lord! Yes, God had great plans for these three girls!

Uncle Alex led the way up to the fourth floor—all of us still on tiptoe to avoid even the slightest noise. When we got to the door that went out to the rooftop landing,

Alex put his finger to his lips, signaling us to be quiet. He inched open the door, peered out the crack, and then eased it closed again.

"He's over there against that wall," he whispered, pointing. "He's looking down toward the street. It's perfect. I don't think he suspects anything."

"Why don't we just shoot him and be done with it?" Bonehead asked.

"You seem to be forgetting our plan," I whispered sternly. "Remember now, only disarming—no killing."

Uncle Alex whispered, "Okay, once again, here's the plan, so we'll be sure we've got our signals straight. To get him coming our way, Bonehead and Dry Bones, you open the door about a foot. Scream; taunt; but no cursing. As soon as he turns toward you, slam the door and tear down the steps."

"Suppose he starts shooting?" Bonehead asked. "I mean, if he suspects we're Hidden Skulls, he'll shoot to kill!"

"That's where you've got to be quick," Uncle Alex responded. "As soon as you slam that door, take off. He may even fire at the door. Don't wait around to see. You head for Cecelia's room. One thing in your favor is that it's darker in here than it is out there."

Then Uncle Alex pointed down the stairs and said, "That's where I'll be—just inside the door at the bottom of these stairs. Marji, you go down one more flight and be looking up. As soon as he gets to where I'm standing, you open fire. Now fire up toward the ceiling. Don't fire up the stairs, or you might hit him or me. All I want is for the gunfire to startle him. When you start shooting, he'll crouch. Then I'll open that door right behind him."

He looked at me, wondering whether I would be able to get it right. "Now Marji," he said, "it's very important that you don't open fire until he gets to that landing. And when he hits that landing, don't delay, because if he starts down the next flight of stairs, we'll lose him. And if you start firing too soon, he's going to stop where he is, and there'll be no way I can get behind him. Timing is absolutely important."

"Alex, are you sure you weren't a general in the army?" Bonehead whispered. "That's a good tactic!"

"Well, I was a platoon leader," he replied. "I never did get to be a general, but I sure got into combat."

"Now I see what you meant when you said we retreat to go forward," Bonehead said.

Uncle Alex eased the door open again and whispered, "He hasn't moved an inch. Boy, is he a sitting duck. I could knock him off easily. But we have to save his soul."

Then he told me to head down the stairs and said to the girls, "When we're in position, I'll give a low whistle. That'll be the signal for you to start in on him."

While we were walking down, Uncle Alex pointed and said, "Okay Marji, you stand down there. When he's coming down the stairs, he won't be able to see that spot. But as soon as you see him, you start firing. And keep firing no matter what happens. If he aims his rifle toward you, he won't have a chance. I'll be on him that quickly."

"Are you sure?" I asked. "You're not as young as you were when you were in the army."

"You seem to forget that God is with us," he told me. "He'll help us."

I walked alone down the next flight, my hands trembling. I had to remember to grab the handle with both hands. I knew I had to start shooting at the right time, or I could cost Uncle Alex his life!

When I got into position, I looked up. Through the darkness, I could just barely see Uncle Alex.

"Are you in position?" Uncle Alex called softly.

"I think so."

"Whatever you do, don't forget to fire at the exact

time," he said again. "If you don't, someone is likely to get killed."

I spread my feet apart and grabbed the gun with both hands. But I was trembling so hard I couldn't hold it steady. And I kept reminding myself to shoot into the ceiling.

I heard Alex's low whistle. Then Bonehead and Dry Bones started screaming and taunting. And Dry Bones cursed! She wasn't supposed to do that! But this was no time to go up and give her a sermon on the evils of cursing!

Then the two of them came flying down the stairs. I heard footsteps running after them. The sniper had to be on his way. I tensed, ready for what lay ahead.

Then I saw his figure at the landing. This was it!

I held the gun above my head with both hands, and squeezed the trigger again and again. The noise resounded through those empty halls, and plaster started sifting down from the ceiling. I saw the sniper stop and crouch. So far so good. Then I saw him aim his rifle in my direction. In another second he would be shooting at me! Should I aim at him? No, Uncle Alex had said not to shoot in that direction.

And it's a good thing I didn't, for I saw Uncle Alex's shadow leap toward the sniper. He must have come down really hard on his back, because I heard the rifle clatter to the floor. Then there was a big scuffle. Then nothing.

I stood there, petrified. What if the sniper had overpowered Uncle Alex? He'd be after me next!

Then a scream broke the stillness, but it wasn't the scream of a Tattooed Terror. It was Uncle Alex's excited yell: "We got him! We got him!"

Bonehead, Dry Bones, and I all ran up the stairs. There was the sniper, out cold! One of the girls picked up his rifle.

Uncle Alex, huffing and puffing, declared, "It was easier than I thought. I think God must have been in my punch."

The sniper started to groan; then his eyes opened. As soon as he saw us, he tried to get up. But Alex jerked the boy's arms behind his back and said, "Keep those guns on him. If he tries anything, we'll. . . ."

He didn't finish the sentence. We knew we weren't going to hurt him, but he didn't know that. I couldn't help but notice how young he was. It was hard to believe he could be a killer.

Uncle Alex kept the sniper's arms pinned behind his back and his own arm around the boy's throat as we marched him down the stairs. Bonehead started to laugh as she said, "Man, if we only had Alex Parker as a member of our gang, we would reign supreme throughout New York City!"

"Come on, girls; we're in the army of the Lord, not in a gang," I said. "Remember?"

Cecelia was waiting for us in the hallway. "Wow, that was quick!" she exclaimed. "I guess God really must be on your side."

It was easier to find our way down with the candle she carried, and soon we were out in the street. Suddenly it occurred to me that we had a problem. Sure, we had disarmed the sniper, but what were we going to do with him? We couldn't keep him in captivity forever!

"Young man, what is your name?" Alex asked, as we paused by the door outside our tenement.

"Broken Bones."

"Broken Bones?" Dry Bones asked in amazement. "Hey, man, what are you doing? I didn't know you were a member of the Tattooed Terrors!"

"Yeah, man, they got me one night and threatened to kill me if I didn't come over to them."

"Marji, you'll never believe this, but this character used to belong to the Hidden Skulls," Dry Bones explained. "It's a good thing I became a Christian tonight. If I had killed Broken Bones, my gang would have promoted me to a warlord! I mean, I'd be the big dude in the gang! You're really lucky, Broken Bones."

The boy looked terror stricken as he asked, "What are you going to do with me now?"

"Nothing. Absolutely nothing!" Alex replied. "If we had wanted to kill you, we could easily have done it up there." He pointed to the roof. "When you were leaning over the side, I could have quickly put a bullet in the back of your head. You never would have known what hit you. But young man, you're safe. You've had an encounter with Christians. Jesus taught us to love our enemies."

Broken Bones's mouth flew open. "You mean you're not going to kill me?"

Uncle Alex laughed. "No. And we're not even going to turn you in to the police. As I said, young man, we're Christians. And we'd like for you to be one, too."

Broken Bones stared, looking from one of us to the other in total disbelief at what was happening. "This is crazy, man, crazy! Nothing like this ever happened to me before."

Alex released his grip, and Broken Bones slowly started to back away.

I looked at the girls. Dry Bones had her fists clenched. Bonehead's finger was tightening on the trigger of the rifle. They wanted to pounce on Broken Bones. That old gang nature was still there. God would have to deal with that.

I went over and gently took the rifle from Bonehead and handed it to Cecelia. "You'd better hold this for a while," I told her.

Broken Bones kept backing up. "If I start running, is anybody going to shoot?" he asked.

I aimed my gun toward him, and he screamed, "Don't kill me, man! Don't kill me!"

Keeping the gun trained on him, I said, "I just want you to remember one thing. Someday when you're all alone, I want you to thank God that He's kept you alive. My uncle could easily have killed you. I could pull this trigger right now. If this were real gang warfare, you'd be dead. But I want you to get this message. God's got a beautiful plan for your life. He doesn't want you killed. And I want you to know that I didn't set up your gang with the police. I'm your friend."

Cecelia kept murmuring, "I'm dreaming. I'm dreaming."

"Remember, you tried to kill us," I said, "but we could easily have killed you, and we didn't. Don't ever forget that!"

I lowered the gun. "Okay, you can go now."

No sooner were those words out of my mouth than he took off like a jaguar! He zigzagged back and forth because he was so positive that somebody was going to start shooting at him. And he disappeared around the first corner he spotted.

"Boy, is he ever lucky," Dry Bones said. "If I'd been holding that gun, I'd have let him have it. That guy's a killer and a traitor."

I got the impression from her inflection that the latter was a far more serious crime to gangs than the former.

"Do you know where he's headed?" Bonehead asked.

"Where?"

"Right to their headquarters. He's probably going to get the rest of the gang. They'll be back here in five minutes."

"I guess we don't need to worry about that," I responded. "Remember? The rest of them are still in jail."

Then it hit me. I'd asked the mayor to release them. Maybe he'd done it. If that sniper found them, they'd surely be heading this way, and there would be no stopping them. It hadn't taken me long to find out that these gangs simply didn't listen to reason. Had we made a serious mistake in letting Broken Bones go?

We had to move quickly now, so we hurried Cecelia up to the apartment, where Aunt Amilda immediately took over by fixing the poor girl the first nourishing food she'd had in ages. I knew she wouldn't be able to eat much. But maybe her kicking was almost over. Amilda would pray for her, too.

Alex and I and the two girls decided we'd better head for the Hidden Skulls' headquarters right away, although they seemed shaky about going. I reassured them that God had everything under control.

"I don't know," Bonehead said, "whether I want to be a live chicken or a dead hero. I know everything is going to break loose when we take you in there, Marji. And when Dry Bones and I tell them we're leaving the gang, that will be it. I mean, it'll be all over!"

"Now come on, Bonehead," I said, "I believe God will save the leader of your gang and the warlords. Then great peace will come to this area."

Dry Bones laughed. "That'll be the day! That'll be the day!"

About half a block from the headquarters, Bonehead stopped. "Are you two still armed?" she asked.

"We sure are," we echoed in unison.

"Well, that's a problem. As soon as we go inside, they're going to frisk you. If they find those guns, they'll never believe a word we say. You'd better give me those guns."

"What?" Alex protested. "I have to give up my gun?"

"Do you want to take the chance?" Bonehead asked. "Listen, if you want to take that chance, you'll be the loser. I'm doing this for your own good. Now give me the guns."

We both handed over our weapons. "The gun belt, too," she said.

I unbuckled it, saying, "I really didn't think I'd have to get rid of this award so soon."

She took the whole arsenal, opened a nearby garbage can, and threw them in with all the stinking garbage. I tried to remember which garbage can it was. Maybe I could get the gun back later. We had left Broken Bones's rifle up in our apartment, so we didn't have to try to stash that.

As we walked on, I felt a little insecure without my gun. Uncle Alex seemed nervous, too. But I also knew I didn't want to become dependent on a gun for protection.

Dry Bones pointed toward a burned-out tenement. "That's it," she said. "As soon as we go down the stairs, two guys will be standing there, both armed. But don't be afraid. Let me handle it."

As we neared the entrance, my heart again beat wildly. What would happen down there? Then I glanced down the street. I couldn't believe my eyes. A whole gang was heading for the same place we were. And at the head of the gang was a familiar figure—Ratface. And right beside him was Broken Bones! The Tattooed Terrors were out of jail. The mayor had found a way to do it! But here they were, heading our way, looking for blood!

14

As soon as Ratface and the Tattooed Terrors spotted us, they started running toward us. "Quick! Into our headquarters!" Dry Bones ordered.

The four of us flew down those steps underneath the tenement, right by the two guards, as Dry Bones yelled, "It's on, man; it's on! The Tattooed Terrors are out in the street!"

We burst through a door as gang members scattered all over the place. "We're on, man! We're on!" Dry Bones kept screaming. "The Tattooed Terrors are out on the street!"

Every gang member leaped to his feet. Some pulled out their switchblades; others pulled out zip guns and revolvers. Then it was as if Uncle Alex and I weren't even there. They all pushed past us toward the battle on the street. I'd come hoping to preach the Gospel to these young people. Now we were right in the middle of a war!

Dry Bones had pulled her switchblade, too, so I grabbed her arm, pleading, "Please don't do it. Christ has come into your heart. This is the time to resist those forces of evil that make you want to fight."

She tried to pull away. "Don't you understand, Marji? It's me or them! They've come to kill! If we don't kill them, they'll kill us. They have no mercy!"

"Please, Dry Bones, listen to me. God will settle this war between the gangs. If you call yourself a Christian, you'll set the cause of Christ back if you don't act like one. Now drop that knife!"

My stern voice surprised even me. Dry Bones stared at me. "Drop it!" I repeated.

She released her grip, and the knife clattered to the floor. I picked it up and threw it over into a corner.

Now where was Bonehead?

I spotted her, carrying a switchblade and heading toward the street.

"Bonehead," I called, "I just talked to Dry Bones. She's with us. She's on God's side. Drop your switchblade, too. Please don't take it up and kill. That's not God's plan for you, for Dry Bones, for me, or for either of these gangs."

She paused and looked toward me.

"Drop it and join us in prayer," I pleaded. "I need you to help me pray. Only God can stop this war!"

Bonehead smiled. Then she took her switchblade and threw it as far as she could.

We were the last ones out of the headquarters. As we peered up to the street, I could see people crouching behind garbage cans. Others had hurriedly set up barricades. Down the street, the Tattooed Terrors were getting ready for the assault.

Uncle Alex dropped to his knees on the steps and started to pray. I mean, he was really in earnest!

I dropped down beside him and said, "Uncle Alex, what are we going to do?"

"I don't know," he responded. "I've never been in a mess like this before. I figured the best thing to do was to pray. God will have to help us out of this one. But I sure don't know how He's going to do it!"

The first shot split the air. Then another. Then another. The war was on!

Suddenly the Spirit of God came strongly upon me, giving me superhuman courage, and before I knew what was happening, I found myself running right out into the street, right in the middle of that gun battle! Everything grew deathly quiet. I pointed toward the Tattooed Terrors and yelled, "In the name of Jesus, I come to you as a messenger of God. These gang wars and killings must stop! Lay down your arms in the name of Jesus!"

You expected it happened, right? Wrong. You have never heard such an outburst of laughter as roared forth from the Tattooed Terrors. Then someone yelled, "Hey, preacher lady, say your prayers because we're going to get you!"

There was another roar of laughter. They thought it was hilarious. But I didn't! There was no mistaking the spiritual power I felt, there in that street. I didn't wonder at all. I knew I was right where God wanted me to be, doing what He wanted me to do. I don't know how I knew it; I just did—as surely as I have ever known anything.

I whirled around and pointed toward the Hidden Skulls and yelled: "Jesus Christ, the Son of the living God, has a greater plan for you, a plan of peace. Lay down your arms!"

No one replied from that side of the battlefield. I knew Dry Bones and Bonehead were out there somewhere with them. But at least they had already laid down their arms. That was a victory!

Once again I faced the Tattooed Terrors. Then I started walking toward them—right toward Ratface. I moved right up to him, wagged my finger in his face, and said, "Call this war off now! God is in this street tonight. He has spared my life to bring you a message of hope. I know you think I set you up in your headquarters, but I didn't. Ask Broken Bones."

Ratface hissed, "I ought to kill you now, Marji Parker! You've been nothing but trouble to us. I ought to kill you now!"

I threw my arms out and screamed back, "Kill me, then! Kill me! I'm ready to meet Jesus!"

Ratface raised his gun, aiming it right between my eyes. Had I made a foolish mistake? Would he take it as a dare that he had to follow through on or lose the respect of his gang? Was I tempting God? One thing was certain, it was too late to worry about it now. I'd already said it!

"Ratface, Jesus loves you," I called out so everybody could hear. "You may kill me, but you can't stop the war in your own heart. You can kill a thousand Christians— yes, a *million* Christians, but that still won't stop the war! *You* have to stop it! Why don't you let Jesus come into your heart and change all that now?"

Ratface stared at me through eyes filled with evil and hate. His finger quivered. One squeeze on that trigger, and I would fly into eternity.

Then I noticed that this man of steel nerves was starting to tremble—so much so that he had to put his other hand on his gun to keep it steady!

Slowly lowering the gun, he sobbed, "I can't do it! I can't do it!"

Then I heard someone weeping in the background, the same as when I was at the gang's headquarters.

Here came Tarzan—big old Tarzan—making his way through the gang to drop to his knees beside me. "Pray for me, Marji," he pleaded. "I have to get right with God. I know God is here. That had to be God who kept Ratface from pulling that trigger. That had to be God. I know it!"

I put my hand on Tarzan's head and said, "Yes, Tarzan, He surely is here. Ask Him right now to forgive your sins; He'll take you back. Cry out to Him."

Over to my right, another gang member dropped to his knees. To my left, I saw Broken Bones on his knees. Then three more members knelt down. As I watched, one by one, almost every Tattooed Terror dropped to his knees and began crying out to God for mercy and forgiveness! What a miracle!

Then I heard something metal clunk at my feet. I glanced down and saw a switchblade. Then more and more. The gang members were all throwing their guns and knives into a pile at my feet.

"Ratface, God is giving you what may be your last opportunity," I said solemnly. "Your life isn't worth much out here on this street. Why don't you kneel with the rest of your gang and take Jesus as your Saviour? He wants to forgive and cleanse you, too."

Trembling all over, he cried, "I can't. I'm too awful to become a Christian."

I put my arm around him and said, "Ratface, do you know why you're trembling so?"

"I've never been afraid of anybody in my whole life," he sobbed. "Now I'm so scared. What is it?"

"That's the Spirit of God convicting you of your sins. He's trying to break through that cold, hard heart of yours and put in the love of Jesus."

Ratface fell to his knees and cried out, "Jesus, save me!"

Uncle Alex came over and dropped to his knees beside Ratface. I dropped to my knees, too, and said, "Jesus is here right now. Just ask Him to forgive your sins and come into your heart. He'll do that, right here on this street."

I looked around and could hardly believe what I was seeing. Every Tattooed Terror seemed to be praying. God had indeed worked a miracle!

Down the street, the Hidden Skulls were simply standing there, nonplussed. If they had wanted to, they could have started shooting and massacred the Tattooed Terrors. They had no idea what was going on. But I believe God restrained them from starting anything. Now if they would just listen. . . .

Then we heard the sirens getting closer and closer, and police cars appeared from everywhere. Suddenly the Tattooed Terrors were on their feet, scrambling to get away. "Nobody run!" I screamed. "Nobody run! Let's believe God!"

But the Hidden Skulls quickly took off.

One police car roared up to where I was standing. Out jumped Captain Wiley. Policemen everywhere had guns trained on the Tattooed Terrors. Was it all going to come to naught again?

"Parker, what's going on here?" Captain Wiley yelled.

"Captain, you may not believe this, but we were having a prayer meeting out here in the street."

"Church? You're having church in the middle of the street?"

"Well, you know these gang members. I couldn't get them into church, so I brought the church to them." I turned toward the gang members. They all nodded and laughed.

"Hallelujah!" Ratface yelled. Then they all started yelling, "Hallelujah!"

Over to the side of the street, one of the officers was yelling it, too: "Hallelujah!" Then another: "Hallelujah!"

I looked at Captain Wiley and said, "Well, captain, aren't you going to join us?"

He threw up his hands and yelled, "Hallelujah!" It was good to see a police captain give God credit for something he knew no human power could accomplish.

Windows all along the street started popping open. People peered out and yelled, "Hallelujah!"

"I don't believe this, Parker," Captain Wiley said. "I just don't believe this! Whatever you've got and whatever you've done, I think I need it, too."

"Would you take these weapons with you?" I asked. "These young people won't be needing them anymore."

He shouted an order to a couple of officers to pick up the guns and knives. Then he yelled, "Let's go, men, it looks as though everything's under control here!"

Even though it was late, I gathered all the Tattooed

Terrors around me and marched them to my counseling center. There, I took my Bible and explained to them, step by step, how to be saved. It was such a beautiful experience to see those young people eagerly reaching out for spiritual help. And Christ did save them.

The next day I took Bonehead, Dry Bones, and Cecelia up to the Walter Hoving Home, where they did remarkably well in the program.

Several times a week I met for Bible study and prayer with the members of the Tattooed Terrors. Then they joined a local church, where they really grew in the Lord.

The Tattooed Terrors no longer exist as a gang on the Lower East Side. The gang completely disbanded after that miracle on the street. That was two years ago. Some of the gang members are now Bible-school students. In fact, just the other day one of them wrote to me that he wants to come back and help me in my work. I can hardly wait for that day.

Bonehead's and Dry Bones's conversions really shook up the Hidden Skulls. Those girls are in Bible school now, too. But the Hidden Skulls still exist as a gang, and I keep praying for them. The conversion of the Tattooed Terrors didn't turn the Lower East Side into heaven. It didn't even bring the sweeping revival that I had hoped and prayed for. But God is still working. I know there's nothing too difficult for Him.

Right now, I'm concerned about you. Did you know that God has a plan for your life? Did you know the Bible talks about you? It says that God has good plans for you. And just as He saved all those members of the Tattooed Terrors, He wants to save you, too. You can be free from that load of sin and guilt. All you have to do are three very simple things:

1. Admit that you're a sinner. You know that. I don't even have to try to convince you of that.

2. Ask Jesus to forgive your sins. Remember, you

don't have to name them individually. Just ask Him to forgive them all.

3. Accept Him by faith into your heart and life. Look up Romans 10:9, 10 and read it, just as Uncle Alex did for Bonehead and Dry Bones.

You don't have to be a gang member to need Jesus. Everybody needs the Saviour. So if you really want joy and peace and forgiveness and freedom from guilt, if you really want a purpose for living, follow those three simple steps. It works!

Remember, only Jesus can stop the war going on in your heart. That's why we call Him the Prince of Peace. So take Him as your Saviour right now. He's waiting to bring His peace into your life, and to get you into the beautiful plan that He has just for you.

The Walter Hoving Home.

Some good things are happening at The Walter Hoving Home.

Dramatic and beautiful changes have been taking place in the lives of many girls since the Home began in 1967. Ninety-four percent of the graduates who have come with problems such as narcotic addiction, alcoholism and delinquency have found release and happiness in a new way of living—with Christ. The continued success of this work is made possible through contributions from individuals who are concerned about helping a girl gain freedom from enslaving habits. Will you join with us in this work by sending a check?

The Walter Hoving Home
Box 194
Garrison, New York 10524
(914) 424-3674

Your Gifts Are Tax Deductible